Escape from the Isle of the Lost

ALSO BY MELISSA DE LA CRUZ

Escape from the Isle of the Lost

A DESCENDANTS NOVEL

#1 *NEW YORK TIMES* BEST-SELLING AUTHOR
MELISSA DE LA CRUZ

BASED ON *DESCENDANTS 3* WRITTEN BY
JOSANN MCGIBBON &
SARA PARRIOTT

DISNEY • HYPERION
LOS ANGELES   NEW YORK

First Edition, June 2019
10 9 8 7 6 5 4 3 2 1
FAC-020093-19109
Printed in the United States of America

This book is set in Adobe Caslon, Adobe Caslon Pro/Monotype;
Albyona English No. 1/SIAS; Harlean/Laura Worthington;
Linger On/Gustav & Brun
Designed by Marci Senders

Library of Congress Cataloging-in-Publication Data on file.
ISBN 978-1-368-02005-3

Reinforced binding

Visit www.DisneyBooks.com
and www.DisneyDescendants.com

For Mattie

And the

C.H. Class of 2025

who were there from the beginning.
Love you kids.

And for the Shallmans:

Ariana Rose
Nina Juliette
Benjamin Joseph
Jonah Samuel

Thanks for all your support!

Escape from the Isle of the Lost

Some Time Ago . . .

Rude Awakening

Once upon a time in ancient Greece, there lived extraordinary heroes and powerful gods, and the most powerful of them all was *Hades*. Yes, you read that right: *H-A-D-E-S*. Hades gazed over his divine kingdom from high above on Mount Olympus with a smug smile. Life was good. Nope, life was better than good. Life was great! No more working himself to death down in the Underworld. No more living near the smelly River Styx, no more listening to the obnoxious wails and cries of torment from the floating dead all around him. No more living in caves with demons. He had won! He was the greatest god who had ever breathed life into a flying horse! Okay, so he hadn't actually done that yet. But he would soon!

For now, he was more than content to eat plump, juicy grapes fed to him by beautiful nymphs, listen to tinkling music played on lyres and harps, and lounge on a puffy cloud, while his back pocket was full of lightning bolts he could use against anyone who dared oppose him.

He sighed in satisfaction and took a bite from the nearest grape.

Then he spat it out.

"DEAR ZEUS, WHAT ON EARTH WAS THAT?!" he said, choking and gasping for breath as he looked around for water. He took a huge gulp from a dirty mug he found next to him. That wasn't a grape he'd eaten. It was a disgusting, withered raisin that was way past its expiration date! And he wasn't lounging on a cloud at all, but lying on garbage bags! The horror! The humiliation! What was this?! Where was he?!

Hades blinked his eyes. He looked all around. He was in the middle of a crowded bazaar, filled with ruffians of all kinds hawking their sordid wares. There was a tent filled with broken electronics, and another selling old furniture, the merchant sitting in a cracked bathtub. This was no Mount Olympus! Not even close!

He groaned in despair, realizing he had once again dozed off and dreamed he was back where he belonged. He should be up in the sky with his fellow deities—hanging out with vain Apollo, snarky Hermes, and beautiful Aphrodite. . . . But in reality, he was still here. *Trapped.* Stuck on the Isle of the Lost—which certainly sounded like a region in the Underworld if he'd ever heard one—living among a bunch of filthy mortals. (Some of them might *look* like scruffy demons, but they were definitely human.)

The island was surrounded by an invisible barrier that kept him and everyone else there barred from the mainland and unable to use their powers. How long had he been here? Too long! No matter, no matter. He would take care of that soon enough. He had found something among his meager possessions just that morning.

He might not have a pocketful of lightning bolts like his annoying brother Zeus, but he still had his ember. His greatest weapon. An ember that, once sparked, could unleash the fires of doom. He reached into his back pocket, checking to make sure it was still there. Yep. There it was, just a plain lump of coal. He had a plan. He was going to escape, and he was going to escape today.

He felt smug at the proposition. While these filthy losers had to stay here, he would be out among the gods once more! This neglected, remote island was certainly no place for someone who was practically a rock star! He was meant to be worshipped, feared, and admired! Not stepped over and pushed aside by ruffians trying to get to the market before it ran out of brown bananas.

Hades left the crowded bazaar and walked all the way

out of town, to the edge of the coastline. In the distance, he could catch a glimpse of Auradon's gleaming skyline. Somewhere, over there, was his true home. Somewhere, over there, were magic and power and freedom.

He held up his ember. "RELEASE ME!" he yelled to the skies.

The skies did not thunder. Lightning did not strike. Nothing happened.

A few residents of the Isle of the Lost walked by, but they gave him no notice. No one even cared to watch. But Hades would show them! He was just out of practice. He warmed the ember in his hands and then held it up again.

He could feel one of his raging tantrums building. His face began to turn red all the way to the roots of his hair. He needed to get out *right now*. It was time to blow this joint. He was the god of fire and rage, a ruler of souls, one who had brought the mighty Hercules to his knees! (Well, not really—but he *almost* brought Hercules down. Almost!)

"RELEASE ME!" he commanded.

Nothing.

He tried again. . . .

Nothing.

His face turned an even darker shade of crimson and he screamed his anguish toward the sky, throwing curses and hexes every which way.

But still nothing. Hades's shoulders slumped. He was out of breath and out of energy. His blue Mohawk wilted.

He looked down at the ember in his hands. It was dead. It was a piece of coal. It did not glow, nor did it burn with divine fire. It was useless.

Try as he might, and as hard as he wished it otherwise, the reality was that there was no magic on the island. And while that barrier stood, there never would be. Zip. Zilch. Nada. Which meant he had to accept it. On the Isle of the Lost, Hades was no longer a god.

He was just a blue-haired dude in a leather jacket.

Heroes and Villains

"We were so
close! So close
we tripped on
the finish line."
—Hades, Hercules

chapter

1

The Lady Is a Villain Kid

Mal made her way across the sparkling campus of Auradon Prep, taking in the sound of chirping birds, the warmth of the sun against her face, and the sight of the tall castle walls shining with early morning dew. Although Mal wasn't about to burst into song at any moment like some of the princesses and princes who filled this place, she might as well have been singing in her heart. They'd made it! Mal, Evie, and Jay were seniors now—Carlos, who was a junior, still had one more year to rule the school—and in a few months, they would graduate. They would be free to make their own futures, forge their own paths—the world was their pearl-bearing oyster.

As Mal greeted her friends who were milling about the lawns, she recalled their days on the Isle of the Lost. Not so long ago, Mal had spent her free time spraying graffiti on posters featuring King Beast's face with her signature tag: EVIL LIVES. Not so long ago she had been proud of the many, many ways she was wicked. At Dragon Hall, she had been famous for her pranks, locking first-years in their Davy Jones lockers, starting epic spoiled-food fights in the cafeteria, and threatening everyone with Maleficent-style curses if they dared defy her. But it turned out that being evil meant feeling small and petty, while being good meant being brave. It meant facing your fears and standing up for the people who depended on you. Being good was so much harder and so much more satisfying than being bad. It *felt* good to *be* good. Who knew?

Now Mal was Auradon's hero and protector, ready to transform into her dragon self to defend the kingdom against any villain or monster that would threaten its shores. Life had been calm since Uma had disappeared during Cotillion. There had been no sign of that turquoise-haired sea witch so far. Mal's childhood rival had dived deep into the waves, and had not been seen since. But Mal liked to keep watch anyway. You never knew where or when the enemy would strike.

"Any sign of her?" she asked the guard, who had been stationed by the coastline to check.

"Not today," the guard replied.

"Good," said Mal.

When she arrived at the meeting for the Royal Council, she was the first one there. Today she was dressed simply in a matching black-and-purple shirt and skirt, her long purple hair tucked behind her ears. Gone were the days when Mal would stomp into class or any assignation at the last minute, snarling and annoyed. She was the future Lady Mal now—bad fairy heritage, irreverent attitude, battered thick-soled boots, and all. She wanted to make Ben proud of her, and, in turn, show the kingdom she was proud to wear his school ring.

Still, Mal's unexpectedly prompt appearance seemed to surprise Lumiere, who was still fluffing cushions and helping Cogsworth and Mrs. Potts set out the tea service.

"Oh! Mal! You're early!" said Lumiere with a bit of a frown. As the head of the king's household, he didn't like to be caught with his candelabras down, so to speak.

"Don't mind me," said Mal. "Anything I can do to help?"

"No, dear. Please, be our guest," said Mrs. Potts, bustling over with two heaping plates of scones and pastries, almost dropping them in her haste.

"Here," said Mal, taking one of the plates away from the overburdened cook and placing it in the middle of the table.

"Thank you, dear," said Mrs. Potts with a relieved smile.

"We don't have much time!" fretted Cogsworth, who was opening drapes and letting light into the conference room. "The kings and queen will be here shortly! And Fairy Godmother runs a tight ship. She'll turn us all into pumpkins—or worse, back into furniture—if things aren't perfect!"

"Oh, Cogsworth, you worry too much!" Mal laughed as she helped Chip pour tea into everyone's cups. She knew Cogsworth was simply being his normal, nervous self—Fairy Godmother was far too kind to turn anyone into furniture. After they were done with the tea, she helped Chip fold the napkins the way Lumiere taught them, so they resembled ladies' fans on the plates.

At last, the room was ready, and at the appointed hour, Mal took her seat as Cogsworth held the door open for King Beast, Queen Belle, King Ben, and Fairy Godmother, who all filed in. They were already deep in discussion.

"I think it's a wonderful idea," Ben was saying. "She'll be so thrilled."

"I thought she might," said Fairy Godmother, who looked as polished as ever in her pink ruffled shirt and powder-blue suit.

Ben grinned and took his seat next to Mal.

"Oh, the tea looks lovely, Mrs. Potts," Fairy Godmother said, as she picked up her cup. Cogsworth audibly sighed in relief.

"One lump or two?" asked Chip, appearing at her elbow, as Mrs. Potts beamed behind him.

"What's going on?" whispered Mal to Ben.

"You'll see," he promised, reaching for a scone.

King Beast and Queen Belle, who had recently returned from another all-kingdom cruise—they had become very fond of those—looked deeply tanned and relaxed. Ever since handing over the reins of government to their son, the retired king and queen were only brought in to consult with the Royal Council. Ben had the final word on every decision.

Ben let the assembled group eat and chat for a moment before calling the meeting to order. "Mal, I'm sorry we started this discussion· without you, but it's come to my attention that some members of the Royal Council would like for you to do some diplomatic visits around all the kingdoms of Auradon," he explained. "I think you would do an amazing job. What do you think?"

"Oh!" said Mal, sitting up straighter. "That sounds . . . exciting!"

"I thought you would say that!" Ben smiled at her, but then his brow creased. "Although it *does* mean a lot of travel," said Ben. "And frankly, I'll miss you."

In the back, Mrs. Potts swooned while Chip giggled.

"Ben," said Mal, taking his hand at the table. "I'll always come back to you."

Ben smiled back and squeezed her hand. He had grown up so much since the crown was first placed on his head.

He was their leader, fair and firm, and so handsome that she still blushed when he looked her way. "I'll be waiting," he promised.

Fairy Godmother cleared her throat. "It's important that our future *Lady* Mal see as much of the kingdom as she can. She didn't grow up in Auradon, and it would be good for her to observe the customs of the country."

"I agree," said Queen Belle. "The people are curious about Mal and excited to show her how much they appreciate all she's done for Auradon. I know in Northern Wei, they're planning a dragon dance parade in her honor. And in Corona, a festival of sky lanterns."

King Beast beamed. "What wonderful news! Dear, do you think our next cruise could take us to Northern Wei as well? I've never even seen a dragon dance myself!"

"I'll make sure of it," said Queen Belle.

"Then it's settled," said Fairy Godmother. "I hope it's not too distracting from your studies, my dear. But here is a list of kingdoms for your itinerary." She pushed a piece of paper across the table in Mal's direction.

Mal felt her heartbeat speed up in excitement. It was true—she hadn't seen very much of Auradon at all, and the chance to travel the world sounded thrilling after a childhood spent trapped on a remote island. So many things to see! So many people to meet!

She glanced at the list.

Agrabah, Camelot, Northern Wei, Olympus, East Riding, Corona . . . and everywhere else, from Tiger's Head to Triton's Bay. So many wonderful places to visit! She couldn't wait to eat beignets with Princess Tiana's family and sip nectar and honey with the gods and goddesses in their palace in the sky. Every kingdom and region in Auradon was represented on her itinerary.

Every region, that is, except one.

Mal looked up from the paper. "Did we forget to add the Isle of the Lost to this list?" she asked.

"The Isle of the Lost?" echoed Fairy Godmother, as if she couldn't quite believe her ears.

King Beast and Queen Belle shifted uncomfortably. King Beast coughed, and Queen Belle added two more lumps of sugar to her tea. When she brought the cup to her lips, it rattled against the saucer she held underneath it.

"The Isle of the Lost is Mal's home," Ben reminded everyone.

"Yes, it is," said Mal. It was her duty to represent the island as much as she could, to remind everyone that there were noble hearts everywhere, and that even villain kids could grow up to be good. "And the Isle is part of Auradon, right?"

"Technically," Fairy Godmother admitted.

"Unfortunately," groused King Beast.

"Now, now, dear," said Queen Belle.

"Then shouldn't I visit the Isle as well?" she said. "Shouldn't I go there as part of my official itinerary? I don't want them to think they've been forgotten." It was already so easy to dismiss the kids who were imprisoned on the island, punished for their parents' evil deeds. If Ben hadn't felt sympathy for them in the beginning, when he made his first proclamation as king, who knew where she would be now? Certainly not in a plush room in the palace eating warm scones on a porcelain plate. Most likely scrounging for leftovers in back alleys like every other Isle kid.

"Of course not," said Ben. "We can't forget the Isle of the Lost."

"Let's not make a hasty decision just yet," said Fairy Godmother. "Why don't we discuss it again at the next meeting of the Royal Council? Give us a little time to think it over."

"Absolutely," said Ben with a smile. "Besides, I'd take any excuse to have more tea and scones from Mrs. Potts."

chapter

2

Arabian Knight

*J*ay and his opponent battled up and down the mat, crashing against the walls and over every obstacle. Once the slyest thief in all the Isle of the Lost, Jay had found that it was just as much fun to score a goal in tourney or win a battle at R.O.A.R. as it was to swipe a scarf from a merchant on the plaza. Maybe even more fun, since no one chased him around angrily afterward. Whenever he put on his team's yellow-and-blue face mask or picked up his sword for another round of swords-and-shields practice, he forgot that he had ever spent his childhood in a junk shop on a remote island. All he cared about was victory, his world narrowing to the points he scored against his fearsome opponents.

He leaped and attempted a strike, but was deflected. His opponent rushed forward and made a hit. The referee called the score. Now Jay was behind.

They went back to their places on the mat, and this time, Jay waited and let his rival come to him. He didn't have to wait for long, and was on the defensive again, blocking strikes and cleverly dodging any attack.

At last, he found his advantage, twirled around, and landed a direct hit. The buzzer sounded, signaling that time was up, and the referee blew his whistle. "That's the game," the ref called. "It's a tie!"

"Good one!" said Lonnie as she took off her mask and let her long black hair fall on her shoulders. She shook his hand.

"Thanks, Captain." Jay grinned as he removed his mask and gloves.

There was a round of applause from a group lined up along the courtyard, watching them. "Excellent work!" said one. "Brilliant!" said another. "Bravo!" said the third.

Jay squinted in their direction. He hadn't noticed them at the start of the match. He'd been playing for himself, not to impress anyone. "Who are they?" he asked, as he put his equipment away.

"Coaches," said Lonnie. "It's college visiting day, remember?"

Jay did not remember. He never kept track of dates or read announcements or e-mails. Life was too short, and he had too many fun things to do, like play video games and eat pizza.

"Go over there! They definitely want to meet you," said Lonnie, gently pushing him in their direction.

The first coach was a muscular gentleman in a black-and-gold vest, voluminous white pants, and gold shoes with curled tips. He wore a grand white turban with a ruby in the middle and a gold stripe running around it. "Jay!" he said heartily, as if they were old friends. "I am Coach Razoul, formerly captain of the guard at the Sultan's palace. But now I head up the athletics program at ASU—Agrabah State University."

"Nice to meet you," said Jay, bowing to the coach.

The coach bowed in return, seemingly pleased that Jay remembered Agrabah's customs. "You must come and visit us sometime. Have you decided where you will continue your education? Would you consider coming home?"

Jay startled at that. While his father was from Agrabah, Jay's home was the Isle of the Lost. But he didn't want to embarrass Coach Razoul. "To be honest, I haven't given it much thought yet." Graduation was still a few months away. He didn't have to decide where to go to college yet, did he? Definitely not.

"Jay!" said the next coach, a big bear of a guy who wore

the green livery of Robin Hood's men. "Coach Little John here, from Sherwood Forest University. We'd love to see you play for the Arrows." He handed Jay a card. "We're ranked number one in the league."

"For archery," said Coach Razoul, wagging his finger. "Not R.O.A.R."

"Not yet, maybe," admitted Little John. "But with players like you, we will be."

Coach Razoul gave the archer a condescending smile. "In Agrabah, your dormitory will be a palace! Every meal is a feast, and if you rank first in your class, a genie will grant you three wishes!" He pressed a gold-foil-covered catalog into Jay's hands.

Meanwhile, Little John handed Jay a tote bag filled with Arrows merchandise—a water bottle, a bow and arrow, and a sweatshirt with the school's motto—STEAL FROM THE RICH; GIVE TO THE POOR—embroidered on the front. The bearlike coach smiled affably. "Stealing was your hobby, wasn't it? You'll fit right in!" he said.

"Stealing? Well, in the past maybe. Not anymore. But thank you so much," said Jay, as he accepted the loot.

Not to be outdone, Coach Razoul presented Jay with a treasure chest of riches—robes with the Agrabah State University crest, new golden slippers, and a genie lamp. "It's just an oil lamp, no genie in it," said Coach Razoul with a laugh. "Yet!"

"Don't listen to them," said the third coach, a cheerful

apple-cheeked woman in powder-blue wizard robes with a pink bow that tied the hood under her chin. She looked vaguely familiar. "Hello, Jay! My sister tells me so much about you! You must consider playing for us! Everyone knows MIT is the best college in Auradon. Our alumni include Professor Yen Sid, as well as Flora, Fauna, and Merryweather!"

Magical Institute Training was the top college in the kingdom, taking only the best and brightest from Auradon Prep. Students needed an almost-perfect SAT (Salagadoola Abracadabra Test) to be considered.

"MIT!" said Jay. "I'm not sure I have the grades?"

"Oh, we work miracles at MIT, don't worry," said Fairy Godmother's sister. She waved her wand, and a small white carriage loaded with treats—athletic duffel bags, sneakers, and a new face mask, sword, and gloves—appeared next to the treasure chest and tote bag.

"Think about it." She winked.

"Come home to Agrabah," said Coach Razoul, shaking Jay's hand once more.

"Join our merry band," said Coach Little John, slapping him on the back. "Come to visiting day and hang out with the team."

"Visiting day?" asked Jay. "What's that?"

"Oh, you go on a little adventure with the students, see what Sherwood is like, check out the scene," said Little John. "I think you might enjoy it."

"I think I just might," said Jay with a grin.

"Great! I'll send you the information," promised Little John.

At last, the coaches left to talk to other players. Jay gathered his stuff and jogged back to Lonnie. "Do you want any of this?"

"I'm good. I met with them last week," said Lonnie. "They even spoke to my parents." She picked up the tote bag. "Let me help."

They walked out of the training courtyard together, Jay straining under the weight of the treasure chest and the carriage full of treats. "Did you decide where to apply?" he asked.

"I'm not sure yet if I will. I might play R.O.A.R. professionally instead. But if I do decide to go to college, I'll definitely choose one that would prepare me to join my mother's army. I'm going to be a general like her one day," she said proudly.

"Cool," said Jay. The only inheritance he'd receive from his father was a decrepit junk shop on the Isle of the Lost. But Jafar had been the Sultan's grand vizier once, the power behind the throne. Perhaps one day Jay could have that same kind of stature, but without the greed and the obsession with Aladdin's lamp.

As if she had read his thoughts, Lonnie asked, "What about you?"

"Me? I'm just glad I didn't have to steal any of this," he

said truthfully. Until this moment, he hadn't really given much thought to his future. It felt like he had just arrived at Auradon Prep. He was sad to think that soon there would be no more tourney games, no more living with his friends and seeing them every day. Sherwood sounded like a fun prospect—he would definitely have to visit, see what it was like.

They were all growing up so fast. Time was speeding along too quickly. One day he was just a street rat from the Isle of the Lost, and the next he was a top recruit at MIT. Wait until he told his dad! Except Jafar would probably insist that Jay steal all the school's magical secrets. Some things never changed.

chapter
3

Once, There Was a Princess

As Evie sat at her trusty sewing machine and worked on a gorgeous graduation gown for herself, she felt a flutter of sadness in her chest. When she was a kid growing up all alone in a damp and moldy castle, Evie had wanted nothing more than to have a group of friends—to play with, to laugh with, to depend on. But Mal, Jay, and Carlos were more than friends—they were family. Even though their parents had been just as successful at raising children as they had been in executing their evil schemes (read: total failures), the four of them had always been there for each other. But now high school was ending, and graduation would be here before they knew it. It felt like they were all going their separate ways.

Mal had told Evie about her official tour the other day—she would soon be traveling all over Auradon to learn more about the various kingdoms and their people. Jay was always off training with his R.O.A.R. team, and when Carlos wasn't studying, he spent most of his time with Jane. Evie missed her friends.

She felt a tear come into her eye and almost pricked her finger on the needle. She sighed and put the gown away. It was going to be a deep sapphire blue to complement her hair, with a red ruby heart in the middle. Usually the joy of dreaming up and creating a beautiful dress to wear for a fancy event filled her spirit, but today she just felt melancholic.

"What's wrong? Are you crying?" asked Doug, looking up from Mal's desk, where he was practicing his trumpet.

She smiled sweetly at him and brushed away her tears. "No, not really. I was thinking that everything is happening so fast. Didn't I just arrive at Auradon Prep? Now we're graduating."

"Time certainly flies," he said. "Even my hair is longer!"

She chuckled. Doug had been growing out his hair so that it was shaggier than usual. "It really is!"

"Do you not like it?" he asked worriedly.

"I love it!" said Evie, clasping her hands. "You look very dashing. But . . ."

"But . . . ?" Doug asked, setting down his trumpet.

"But things are ending," said Evie. She hung up her graduation gown and admired its sweetheart neckline and puffed sleeves. Just a few more flourishes on the sash and the dress would be done. "I don't even know where I'm going to live when I graduate. I just realized I don't have a home here. Where am I going to go?" She couldn't return to the Isle of the Lost, of course, but after she left her room at the school dorms, there wasn't anywhere else she could go.

Doug shook his head. "Auradon is your home."

"I know," said Evie. "But I'm not like the other kids. I'm not from here."

"We'll think of something," said Doug, a serious look on his face.

Evie nodded. "I would love to have a place of my own. But who knows what next year will bring?"

"Hopefully not Uma," said Doug.

"Roger that," said Evie, shuddering. "But I *am* hoping next year brings more villain kids to Auradon. You know, to study. Like the four of us."

Doug smiled. "Isn't Ben doing that?"

"Sort of," said Evie. "He definitely wants to recruit more kids from the Isle to apply to Auradon Prep. Except . . ."

"Except?"

Evie smoothed the fabric on her gown. "Well, we're just not getting the response we thought we would."

"How many people have applied from the Isle of the Lost so far?" asked Doug.

Evie turned back to him. "How many?"

"Yeah."

"One."

Doug's mouth quirked in amusement. "One?"

She nodded. "Just Dizzy, who was invited to apply, and actually still has to be selected by the admissions committee before her registration can be confirmed." Evie was sure Dizzy would be accepted, but of course nothing was guaranteed until Fairy Godmother sent the enrollment letter.

Doug crossed his arms against his chest. "Just Dizzy? Really?"

Evie let out a rueful chuckle. "I know. Isn't that sad? There's got to be a way to get more kids from the Isle to apply."

"How many spots are open?" asked Doug.

"Good question. I'm not sure, but I think Auradon Prep would take more than one, since they want more students from the Isle to apply."

"Then what you need," said Doug, putting his trumpet away in its case, "is a recruitment strategy."

Evie looked at him thoughtfully. "Intriguing. Go on."

"The kids from the Isle of the Lost will probably be too intimidated to apply, unless they get encouragement from kids like them who are already doing well in Auradon."

"Kids like us, you mean?" asked Evie, her mind whirling with ideas.

"Exactly. Once they hear more about how you, Jay, Carlos, and Mal have grown at Auradon Prep, they'll be inspired to join you guys. Maybe it won't be so scary if they know they'll be welcome here."

"You're right," said Evie, clapping her hands. "So let's show them! I've got to find Carlos, Jay, and Mal!"

Evie ran from the room, excited to get started. She was halfway down the hall when she realized she'd forgotten something.

Just as quickly, she ran back into her room and kissed Doug on the forehead. "You're a prince. Thank you!"

"Just a dwarf, really, but I'll take it," he said, hugging her back.

chapter

4

Look Out for Carlos De Vil

The last bell of the day had finally rung, and the weekend beckoned. Carlos packed up his books and followed the crowd out of the classroom. There was a lively chatter in the air as people made plans to meet up at Camelot Grill for dinner and darts games or to hang by the Enchanted Lake. He craned his neck and spotted Jane, who had her Advanced Wish-Fulfillment class right next door to his History of Heroism seminar. Carlos was still getting used to the idea that she *liked-him* liked him. He had been so nervous to ask her to Cotillion, she hadn't even understood what he was asking her until it was almost too late. But now, when she saw him, it was like everyone and everything else melted away.

"Hey!" she said, her bright eyes shining. Her dark hair was pulled away from her face with a light-blue headband, and she was wearing a matching ruffled dress. With him in his black jacket, white button-down shirt, and black-and-white pants, they made a handsome pair, if he did say so himself.

They smiled shyly at each other. "Happy Friday!" he said, because seeing her always made him happy.

"Happy Friday to you," she said. They reached for each other's hands at the same time, causing Jane to giggle. "So, is everything set for you-know-what next week?" she asked, lowering her voice in case one of the seniors could overhear them.

"I've got the list, and I've alerted the proper authorities," said Carlos. "Everything should be ready."

"Amazing," said Jane. "It's going to be such a fun night!"

"The best!" he enthused. They had really pulled it together. It had been a little difficult getting all the parents to agree to their plans—Rapunzel, for one, didn't want to let down her hair too much—but in the end they'd all agreed to help. Carlos was no longer the scared little boy who'd arrived at Auradon Prep, shaking at the sight of a puppy. He had grown taller, leaner, and much more confident in the time he'd spent away from the Isle of the Lost. Without his mother's haranguing and constant criticism, he had truly come into his own—especially since he no longer had to fluff her wigs and take care of her furs.

Everything was going happily-ever-after—he was doing well in his classes, he had a very cute girlfriend, and next year, once Jay and Ben had graduated, he was going to be the BMOC: Big Man of the Castle. Maybe he could even run for Class King! He ruffled his crop of black-and-white hair, thinking about how everything would truly be perfect. Except for just one thing—he would miss his friends.

The others would be going their own ways after graduation—that was for sure. Jay was going to be some big R.O.A.R. star, Evie would probably expand her fashion business, and Mal had her duties to Auradon—after all, she was the future Lady Mal now. Carlos felt a tad nostalgic for how it used to be, when the four of them were just a bunch of Isle of the Lost misfits, stumbling and scheming their way through Auradon.

Which was why he was doubly glad he and Jane had coordinated this very special supersecret project next weekend that was part of the traditional graduation activities at Auradon Prep.

"See you tomorrow?" she asked.

· "At the Auradon City Mall," he replied with a grin. "Seven o'clock."

"They just installed new dancing fountains—trained by the Sorcerer's Apprentice!" she said. "It'll be so cool!"

"Can't wait."

He walked her back to her dorm, where she gave him a quick kiss good-bye. "Tomorrow," she promised.

"Tomorrow," he echoed with a smile, still feeling the sweetness of her kiss against his cheek.

As Carlos walked back to the boys' dorm, he texted the group chat nicknamed "VKs":

> C-Dog: *Hey! It's Friday! Let's hang! Want to grab eats at Charming's Chili?*
>
> Malevolent: *Sounds SO FUN, but Ben and I have a dinner with Aziz and his new princess tonight. So sorry!!!*
>
> It'sJay: *Rain check? Kinda sore from practice, spending night in.*
>
> PrincessEvie: . . .

Carlos was waiting for Evie's reply when she ran right into him, still typing a response on her phone.

"Carlos!" she said joyfully.

He broke into a smile; Evie was always so cheerful. She was like a big sister to him. "Evie! What's up? Want to go to Charming's Chili?" he asked.

"I'm so sorry, I can't. Doug's band is playing at the Wishing Well later," she said with an apologetic smile. "Want to come with?" While Doug was a member of the marching band in the daytime, at night he whistled a different tune.

Carlos would usually be happy to join her, except Doug's music was just a tad too *EMO* for him. (Extremely Moody Orchestrations, that is.)

"Next time," Carlos promised, as they fell into step together.

"But do you have time now?" asked Evie. "I'm actually going this way." She motioned back to the main castle.

"Now?" he asked, following her lead.

"Yeah, I was about to go and find Mal and Ben to talk about the VK program—you know, the initiative to bring more villain kids to Auradon?" she asked, as she opened the doors and they stepped through.

Carlos nodded. It sounded vaguely familiar, although he hadn't been paying much attention. Mostly he'd been wrapped up in his new relationship with Jane. "Uh-huh?"

Evie led the way to Ben's private wing of the palace. "I was thinking maybe we should go back to the Isle of the Lost and get more kids interested in applying!"

"We should?" he asked, paling to the roots of his black-and-white hair. Even though they'd returned to the Isle of the Lost before, it always felt like a dicey proposition. In the back of his mind he was always a little worried he'd end up stuck there again, and he really didn't want to be trapped in his dingy room in Hell Hall.

"Yeah, we should!" said Evie, who seemed very intent on this idea. "That way, they can see Auradon is a great

ESCAPE FROM THE ISLE OF THE LOST

place, even for villain kids. Don't you think? Because, so far, no one's applied to the program except for Dizzy."

"Oh." That did seem odd. Carlos would have guessed there would be more kids who might want to escape the island. For starters, he remembered the kids from the Anti-Heroes club were pretty keen on Auradon.

"Yeah." Evie shrugged. "Doug thinks that maybe they're scared or intimidated somehow. Or maybe they think it's some kind of trap. You know how it was, back on the Isle. There's always some kind of angle."

He certainly did. Carlos drummed his fingers on his chin. He was warming up to the idea. "You know what would help? If we brought peanut butter!"

Evie laughed. "Um, okay. I was thinking we should meet with the kids personally to talk about Auradon. But that works too!"

"Perfect. Let's find Jay and Mal first, then go talk to Ben," said Carlos. He always found safety in numbers.

chapter

5

Everyone's Favorite King

Ben bent over the paper on his desk, his brow creased as he read the latest safety report from Genie, who kept an eye on all the kingdoms. The news was the same—no sign of Uma or her tentacles. Ben was writing a note advising Genie to keep an eye on the oceans, when the door to his study burst open. He was surprised but happy to find Mal, Evie, Jay, and Carlos talking excitedly to each other as they made their way to the front of his desk.

"We could tell them about tourney!" said Jay.

"And chocolate chip cookies!" said Carlos. "Oh, and hot showers!"

"We could stress how *good* the classes are. Pun definitely intended," said Mal with a droll smile.

"And how nobody locks you up in a tower if you forget your homework!" said Evie.

"Ben! Wait till you hear this idea!" said Mal, coming to perch on the side of his desk.

"What is it?" asked Ben, grinning and leaning back on his chair, glad to have a distraction. It was his duty as king to read every document presented to him and make certain he was prepared for meetings. He liked to be just as informed as his councillors, if not more so. But sometimes, even kings needed a break. "What's the big idea?"

"You know the VK program?" Evie asked. "The one that's going to bring over some more villain kids to study at Auradon Prep? Well, I was looking at the applications we've received, and aside from Dizzy, there aren't any."

Ben raised his eyebrows. He hadn't heard that it was quite that big a failure. "Really?"

"Yeah, really," said Carlos, taking an empty seat across from Ben's desk. Jay took a place by the windowsill, and Evie sat on a chair near to Mal.

"Isn't that awful?" said Mal. "I think they're scared to apply."

"Or maybe they don't know about it," said Jay. "The Isle is a little . . . isolated."

"So we need to drum up more interest," said Evie. "I was

thinking I could take some photos of us, and we could use them to make posters and put them all over the island. Kind of aspirational! Like, 'You too could grow up to be Mal!'"

Ben smiled. He was pretty sure Mal was one of a kind, but he understood where Evie was going. "Okay, posters. I like it! Maybe we could put them up all around the mainland too, prove to people that anyone can be a great student here."

Mal nodded. "We need to show them that *everyone* can come to Auradon Prep," she said meaningfully.

"Everyone?" asked Ben.

"Well, yeah," said Mal. "Right, Evie?"

"Right," said Evie.

"We'll definitely give everyone a chance to apply," Ben said. "But we can't take everyone from the Isle of the Lost. Where would they live? And who would mentor them? We need to figure out exactly how many kids we can bring over. There's a lot to plan before this happens."

"But we can't waste another day," said Evie.

"I agree," said Ben. "We'll get to work on those posters as soon as possible."

Carlos leaned over. "That's a good start"—he turned to Evie—"but didn't you say you wanted to meet with kids to talk about the program? That the four of us should go to the Isle of the Lost?" His tone was hesitant.

"Well, yes, as long as Ben thinks it's all right," said Evie hopefully. "I just think if we could tell them exactly how wonderful it is here, and answer their questions, we'll be able to get a lot more of them interested in applying."

"The four of you? Back to the Isle?" Ben pondered the idea. The last time they had gone back to the Isle, things hadn't gone so well. As in, getting kidnapped by Uma, and then being tied to the mast of a pirate ship and menaced by some pirate holding a hook in his hand. Ben had sympathy for the kids on the Isle, but he wasn't sure he really wanted his friends to go back there. Wasn't it too dangerous?

He said as much.

"Dangerous? Not to us," scoffed Jay. "We know every trick in the book."

"Because we wrote it," said Mal.

"Danger is my middle name," said Carlos. "I'm serious. Ask my mom. Or Dude. Or neither. Neither might be preferable."

"We can handle it," said Evie. "Nothing will happen."

But there was also Fairy Godmother to think about. "Auradon Prep discourages student travel during the school year," said Ben.

"But not if it's part of my diplomatic visits . . ." mused Mal. "That's it! My diplomatic visits!" She turned to Ben, her eyes sparkling. "We both agreed that the Isle of the Lost should be included on my official itinerary. And if I'm using my visit to promote the VK program at the same time,

Fairy Godmother won't be able to say no. It's the perfect opportunity!"

"And we'll all come too!" said Evie.

"Definitely," said Jay. "You'll need all the help you can get."

"Yeah," said Carlos. "I don't want to see my mother. But I guess I'm in."

"Good," said Mal, who smiled at Evie.

Ben finally nodded. "It does make sense. We'll present it at the next council meeting!"

chapter

They Weren't Kidding When They Called Her, Well, a Witch

*U*ma seethed as she swam under the waves, thinking about all the ways she had been wronged. For a brief moment, back at the Auradon Cotillion, she had been a princess; she had stood on the deck of a magnificent ship, and Ben was hers. He had looked in her eyes with love—sure, he had been spelled, but who really cared? Except in the end, that's all it was—a brief moment. As always, Mal had messed things up for her, and Uma was left floundering in the waves, alone.

What was it Ben had said to her that night? *I know you want what's best for the Isle. Help me make a difference.* He had offered his hand, but she hadn't taken it. Instead, she had returned his ring and swum away. But her rage had not diminished.

Mal! Daughter of Maleficent. Meddlesome, annoying, heroic Mal.

It was always Mal.

Still, Uma had to admit, it wasn't all that bad spending this much time in the ocean. At least, not at first. She'd never had the chance before when she was trapped on the island, behind that invisible barrier. Now the world was hers to explore—the undersea world, that is. She had ventured to the deepest depths, seen ancient creatures of incredible size, swum with fish so big that she spent days lounging on their backs, feeling the sun in her hair and the salt spray on her cheeks. But eventually she'd grown listless and bored.

After all, how many coconuts can one person eat?

(Five hundred and twenty-seven. She had counted.)

Uma missed her pirates, she missed their camaraderie, she missed Harry's smart mouth and his sly banter, she missed Gil's goofy appetites. She had been alone too long, under the sea, in the water, with only sharks for company. And sharks were only entertaining for so long.

She could go anywhere she wanted on Auradon, but Uma found herself drawn back to the Isle of the Lost. She didn't belong among the fresh-faced, good-hearted residents of the mainland. She wanted to be back at Ursula's Fish and Chips Shoppe, making jokes with her crew and scheming to free everyone from the island once and for all. And maybe, just maybe, she wanted to go home. Home was a place where when you showed up, they had to take you in, right? She'd seen something like that embroidered on a random pillow in Auradon, so it had to be true.

Uma spent many days swimming around the waters surrounding the Isle, searching for a hole in the invisible barrier. Days turned into weeks, until she lost count. But Fairy Godmother's spell was too strong. Still, there had to be a way to break it, didn't there? Uma was a witch; she had her mother's seashell necklace and the powers of the sea in her blood.

She drew herself up to her greatest height, transforming into a giant octopus with eight arms, and tried to cast her spells. "BREAK BEFORE ME!" she screamed. She felt the magic pulse in her throat and in her veins. The very skies above the island cracked with lightning and thunder.

"I COMMAND YOU TO BREAK!" she raged.

Nothing happened.

The barrier around the Isle of the Lost stood firm. The villains, including her pirate crew, would be trapped behind that dome forever. There was no way out or in.

Uma returned to her human form and swam away.

Once in a while she glimpsed a few pirates at the coastline and tried to call to them. One afternoon she even spied Harry, stealing another fisherman's catch.

"Harry!" she called. "HARRY!"

But he didn't notice. He just unhooked that unfortunate soul's line and stole away with the bounty.

Another day there was Gil, skipping stones on the beach.

"GIL! I'M RIGHT HERE! GIL!" she yelled.

Gil looked into the distance. "Uma?" he asked. He looked down and found a large seashell. He put the conch to his ear.

"YES! I'M RIGHT HERE!"

But he didn't seem to hear her. Eventually he set the conch down.

The next time she saw the boys on the deck of her ship, she didn't even bother to call out to them. There was no use. It was as if she were as invisible to them as the barrier.

Uma dived down into the depths again. Maybe if she swam deep enough, she would find a place where the barrier ended.

It felt like she had been swimming forever, down and down, cutting across currents and into the dark deep below. And still the barrier held. There was truly no way through the spell.

Except . . .

What was that?

That sound . . .

Was she dreaming, or was it . . . rock music? Coming from the depths below?

chapter

Once Upon a Dance

It had been a few days since Mal, Evie, Carlos, and Jay had approached Ben to discuss the VK program, and Mal was starting to feel a little impatient. Every moment on the Isle of the Lost meant neglect, filth, and abandonment for the kids who lived there. The sooner they got more kids to apply to Auradon Prep, and the sooner they got them off the Isle, the better those kids' lives would be. Evie had brought it up again the other night, and Mal had promised she would ask Ben about it today.

They were at their ballroom dancing practice. And even though Mal wished they were training with swords and shields instead, she kept it to herself. Since she had been announced as the future Lady Mal, she and Ben were expected to lead many dances in countless royal balls around Auradon. There were so many styles to learn—the fox-trot, the waltz, the Viennese waltz (who knew there were two kinds of waltzes?) the quickstep, the mambo, the cha-cha.

Ben was already in the palace ballroom with Merryweather, their instructor. The good fairy was wearing her usual blue gown, blue hat, and blue cape. She eyed Mal's purple dress and smiled.

"Good morning, good morning, King Ben, Mal," she said. "Are we ready for our lesson?"

"We sure are," said Ben heartily. Kingly duties took up so much of his schedule, and Mal knew he was glad for any excuse to spend more time together. Even if that meant learning complicated formal dances. "Shall we?" he asked, offering Mal his hand.

"We shall," she said, her eyes sparkling as she took it.

He swept her into his arms, and they began counting the steps to the waltz.

Ben was concentrating hard on his footwork, and Mal had to make sure she kept in time with the beat. So it was only when Ben swung her around and dipped her that she was able to catch his attention.

"Pardon?" he asked, as Merryweather tapped her wand and music filled the room.

"I was saying—about the VK program—I was thinking we should bring as many kids as possible to Auradon Prep," she told him.

"Wouldn't that be too many?" said Ben, spinning her around.

"What's too many?" she asked, trying not to feel dizzy.

Ben shrugged as his hands drifted back to her waist for the next step. "It's a delicate situation. We need to handle it correctly."

Merryweather tapped them with her wand. "Ben, chin up! Mal, please don't hold your skirt that way."

They adjusted accordingly. "I just wish we could bring them all over," said Mal, as they picked up the dance again.

"I know. I do too," said Ben. "Honestly, I didn't realize the impact of my decision on the kids who weren't originally chosen. I didn't know they took it so personally—like Uma."

Mal made a face. "There's only one Uma," she said.

"I don't think Auradon can handle more than one," he said mildly.

"I agree," said Mal, as Ben twirled her around. "So, how many, then? How many kids will be accepted into the program?"

Ben whispered, "Name a number."

"Ten!"

"Two," he replied teasingly.

She snorted. "Six."

"Three."

"Four," said Mal as she curtsied to him at the end of the waltz.

"Done," said Ben, bowing low with a smile.

"Exactly!" said Merryweather as the music ended with a flourish.

Four more villain kids. It was hardly everyone, but it was a start. She smiled at Ben. "Perfect."

"Oh!" Merryweather clasped her hands together. "You are both lovely dancers!"

chapter

8

A Thrilling Chase

Jay knew that graduating from Auradon Preparatory School was no small feat. And over the years he'd discovered the school offered an array of traditions for its graduating seniors to celebrate the achievement. There was the Senior Tea, presided over by a beaming Mrs. Potts. There was the Senior Ball, rivaling official royal balls in pomp and majesty. There was the Senior Crown Ceremony, where first-years placed golden crowns on the seniors' heads. There was Senior Ditch Day, when everyone left class and spent a day at the water park in Triton's Bay. (Jay had practically stuffed himself full of Scuttle's churros!) There was even an upcoming class trip to the Enchanted Wood and a fancy Senior Dinner two weeks before the last day of school.

No one ever made a big deal of anything back on the Isle of the Lost. Once you graduated from Dragon Hall, they kicked you out the door. (Literally.) In comparison, senior year at Auradon Prep seemed like one big celebration. The school did its best to make everyone's last year special and more memorable, and Jay found he was enjoying every minute of it.

But there was one tradition that had absolutely nothing to do with the administration, and if Fairy Godmother ever caught wind of it, she might wave her wand in annoyance and end the entire practice. So every senior kept quiet about it.

This tradition was called the Senior Quest. (Also known as the Senior Scavenger Hunt, but traditionalists liked to call it by its formal name.)

Ben had spent one afternoon at tourney practice filling Jay in on all the details. All participating seniors met at the tourney field at twilight to get the list of objects and tasks. Whoever completed the quest first would go down in Auradon Prep history—and win a trophy, along with a hundred-dollar gift certificate for a meal at Ariel's Grotto.

The Senior Quest was famous for its daring triumphs over the years: Genie had been made to grant three wishes; the statue of King Beast had been stolen from the commons and placed on the roof; the sword had been pulled from the stone. Even more shrouded in legend were its winners:

Prince Charming was said to have charmed his way through it. Prince Philip had slain a dragon (an illusion crafted by Merlin, of course). Princess Merida had shot the highest arrow up in the sky. A student named Wendy was famous for bringing back pixie dust from Never Land. But one thing was certain: Only the best of the best were named champions.

Once Jay had heard about the quest, he couldn't wait. He wanted his name in the history books. As well as that gift certificate—all the fish fingers he could eat!

When he arrived at the tourney field right at sunset—on his motorbike, no less—all the teams were already gathering. Aziz was at the wheel of his Magic Carpet, a tricked-out car with a superfast engine. Chad was on a white horse, alone. Evie and Doug were hanging out with six of Doug's cousins, waiting for the game to start. Doug's cousins were a fun bunch: Cheerful, Shy, Crabby, Snoozy, Doc the Second, and Gesundheit, who was called Gus for short. Crabby was annoyed he had to be on a team with Gus, who was always blowing his nose, but then, Crabby always lived up to his name. Evie was wishing them all good luck.

Jay didn't see Mal and Ben anywhere, but he knew they wouldn't miss this.

Carlos and Jane were standing at the head of the group. It was tradition for the juniors to coordinate and judge the quest, so while Jay was sad Carlos couldn't participate, he knew his friend had had a blast putting everything together.

He'd heard Carlos and Jane laughing over the list many times leading up to this night.

"Okay!" said Jane, holding up a hand to get everyone's attention. "You guys know the rules. There are no rules! First one back to the goalpost with everything on the list wins!"

Jay pulled his motorbike up next to Lonnie's horse. They had agreed to work together as a team. "What's on the list?" he asked.

"Um, let me see," Lonnie replied. "First: 'Bring back a shard from Cinderella's glass slipper.' That's in the museum, isn't it?"

"No, that's the whole one. We need a piece from the one that broke," said Jay. "That would be in Cinderella's castle."

"Yes!"

Groups of seniors were already beginning to break away from the tourney field, laughing and cheering as the quest began in earnest, while Jay and Lonnie continued working on their game plan. Chad's parents, Cinderella and Prince Charming, lived in a castle in nearby Charmington, Jay remembered. It wouldn't be too hard a ride, although Jay was starting to think that maybe a horse and a motorbike weren't the best modes of transport.

"Should we drive instead?" asked Lonnie.

"For sure," said Jay with a grin. "I know where they keep the royal limo."

They dismounted and bolted to the car. Once Jay was

at the wheel, they sped out of the school grounds, a motor-cade of electric carriages filled with rowdy seniors right behind them.

"So, do you know what you're going to do after?" Jay asked as they zoomed up the main road.

Lonnie was still studying the list. "After we win this thing?"

"No, after graduation."

"I think I'm doing a gap year," she said as she folded the map.

"Is that some Northern Wei thing?"

"No, silly. It's an Auradon thing. Some kids delay going to college to see the world."

"Oh, cool."

"This is our exit," she said, pointing to the sign. "Anyway, I'm still not sure if I'm going to college or going pro."

"Pro?"

"There are some professional R.O.A.R. teams coming to recruit at Auradon Prep soon. You should meet them too!" she said. "That way you'll know all your options."

Jay considered it. He hadn't counted on his hobby becoming a profession, but it sounded like a worthy idea. "When will they be here?"

"Next week. Will you remember this time?"

"I'll try," he said. "Will you remind me?"

She laughed. "Fine. And I think we're here," she said, as they pulled up to a towering castle in the woods.

chapter

9

With New Horizons to Pursue

The next meeting of the Royal Council didn't involve scones, mostly because it was after dinner, but Ben's disappointment was assuaged when he noticed that Mrs. Potts was serving dessert instead. Pies and pudding en flambé. *Yum.* He shared a conspiratorial wink with Mal.

His parents were already at the table with Fairy Godmother. After exchanging a few pleasantries and going over the notes for the upcoming trade meeting, Ben steered the conversation back to the decision about Mal's official itinerary.

"Do we really need to discuss this right now?" King Beast yawned.

"Yes, we do," said Ben. They were already late for the Senior Quest, and if this meeting didn't wrap up soon, he and Mal had no shot at the trophy—or bragging rights.

"Sending Mal to the Isle of the Lost doesn't seem like a terrible idea," said Queen Belle gently. "She is from there, and they are our people too."

Fairy Godmother scraped up the last bit of her pudding en flambé. "I agree with Belle," she said. "It's not a terrible idea—I just worry it might be a dangerous one."

"Mal will have her friends with her. She'll be perfectly safe," said Ben.

"I promise, nothing will happen," said Mal. "In fact," she continued, looking to Ben for encouragement, "I would like to use my trip to help with the initiative of bringing more VKs over to Auradon. I think hearing it directly from me and my friends will help these kids understand how their lives can really change for the better."

"I totally agree," said Ben. "It's time to bring more kids from the Isle to the mainland, and Mal can help us do that."

"The longer they stay isolated and influenced by their parents' evil deeds, the harder it will be for them to ever acclimate to life on Auradon," said Mal. "I should know. When we were brought here, our parents tried to get us to steal Fairy Godmother's wand."

"How can we forget?" said Fairy Godmother.

"But now Mal, Evie, Jay, and Carlos are some of

Auradon Prep's top students," Queen Belle reminded them. "The others will be like them."

"I still have my doubts," said Fairy Godmother.

"Please, trust us," said Mal.

"Trust her," said Ben. "As king, I believe this is the right thing to do." He checked his watch. If they made it out of here in the next few minutes, they still had a fighting chance at winning the quest.

"The king has decided, then," said King Beast. "Hear, hear. Mal will be visiting her homeland."

Fairy Godmother nodded. "Hail to the king. And congrats, Mal. I know you'll have a wonderful trip."

"Good job, son," said his mother. "And well done, Mal."

Ben was relieved they had reached consensus so quickly. "Great! Now that we've all agreed, I've outlined the plan," he told them. "Mal and her team can meet with Dr. Facilier of Dragon Hall and liaise with him to drum up interest in the program. Once we receive all the applications, we'll select four new worthy candidates."

Fairy Godmother pulled out a feathered pen and began scribbling notes. "We'll have the royal press issue a proclamation with the dates of Mal's visit."

"Excellent," said Ben.

"Mal, remember that, this time, you will be traveling as Auradon's representative," said Fairy Godmother.

"I won't fail you," said Mal.

Ben looked at the dates Fairy Godmother proposed. "Oh!"

"What?"

"That's the same weekend that we're having the meeting to discuss the new NAFFA trade agreement," said Ben.

"That's right. The National Association of Far Far Away," said King Beast. "Everyone from Agrabah to Camelot will be there."

Ben turned to Mal. "I won't be able to come to the Isle of the Lost with you. I'm so sorry."

"Don't worry about it," Mal said, giving him an understanding look.

"No one said ruling was easy," Ben said with a sigh.

"That's okay," said Mal with a wicked smile. She lowered her voice to a whisper. "You know what *is* easy?"

Ben raised an eyebrow.

"Winning the Senior Quest! We have to move. The first teams are already at Cinderella's castle! Let's go!"

As Mal and Ben zoomed out of the room, Fairy Godmother turned to the king and queen. "Senior Quest? What's that?"

But Belle and Beast only smiled mysteriously. There were some traditions that were best kept secret.

chapter 10

Hold Your Breath, It Gets Better

"Come on," said Evie, tiptoeing along the castle walls. She and Doug had crossed the moat by bringing down the drawbridge. Now all they had to do was get inside.

Evie picked the lock and swung the door open.

"You do that so well," said Doug, a little nervously.

"You can take a girl out of the Isle, but you can't take the Isle out of the girl," said Evie with a smile. She was never embarrassed about where she came from.

They went inside. The castle was empty, since Cinderella and Prince Charming had agreed to let the kids use their castle for the scavenger hunt and were away visiting Prince Charming's father—the King—and the Grand Duke. The servants had been given the day off in preparation as well. Even though Evie and Doug were sneaking in, it was mostly to avoid the other senior teams. Cinderella just asked that everyone take their shoes off at the entry.

Doug led the way up the grand stairs, the two of them padding lightly in their socks, and quickly found Cinderella's closet. Evie stopped to admire the light-blue gown that Cinderella had worn to that famous ball, where she captured the heart of her prince. She touched its silk folds reverently. "Did I tell you?" she asked Doug. "I had an idea to expand my business. I'm going to design everyone's caps and gowns for graduation."

"That's perfect! Everyone is going to want an Evie's 4 Hearts original," Doug said, kneeling down to look at rows and rows of boxes of glass slippers.

"I hope so!" said Evie, admiring Cinderella's many tiaras.

"You can't graduate without one!" said Doug with a smile. He held up one of the shoe boxes. "Where do you think she keeps the shards of the original shoe?"

Evie tried to think. If she were Cinderella, where would she keep her mementos? They searched everywhere, going up to the attic filled with her old brooms and the basement where the castle cooks kept the cauldrons. But there was no sign of the broken shards of the original glass slipper.

"Maybe we should move on to the next item on the list?" asked Doug.

"Hold on!" Evie said excitedly, as she realized the twist. "Cinderella doesn't have the shards of the slipper. She's not sentimental. After all, she sent the remaining one to the museum. Prince Charming was the one who picked it up when she left it at the ball. I bet it's in *his* closet!"

They ran to Prince Charming's closet. . . . But another quest team had already beat them there.

Ben was looking through the shelves while Mal was pulling out the cape rack. "Oh, hey!" said Mal. "You guys are here too!"

"Slipper shards?" asked Doug.

"Nothing yet," said Ben.

Mal turned to Evie. "Guess what? The Royal Council approved my visit to the Isle! We're all going back to recruit more kids to come to Auradon!"

Evie squealed, and the two of them hugged.

"You know, when the new kids come over, we should do something fun, truly celebrate them. Maybe not just the marching band, but an entire parade. A really big welcome!" said Evie.

"That's a great idea," said Doug.

"I like it," said Ben. "Certainly for their first day of school. But we're going to bring the new kids over during the summer, so that they have time to get used to Auradon." He turned over a treasure chest full of medals. "No shards here."

Mal and Evie looked through the prince's collection of crowns. "But where will they stay? The first-year dorms are being remodeled this summer," said Mal.

"We'll find a place!" said Evie cheerfully. She picked up one of the golden crowns and checked underneath it. "Except we can't seem to find any shards of glass."

Mal peeked beneath an ermine coat, where she discovered a safe. "Look!"

The safe was already open, and there was a note on the floor in Jay's handwriting. "'Left you some shards, but the crown is ours!'" Mal read. "He got here first, that thief!"

She reached into the safe and found the velvet bag where Prince Charming kept the shards of his true love's glass slipper. Mal picked up a shard and carefully put it in a plastic pouch. Evie did the same. Then the two teams went their separate ways. Now they just needed to steal a banana from Tarzan's pal Terk's refrigerator. . . .

chapter

11

An Endless Diamond Sky

*I*t was close to midnight. Carlos and Jane sat at the edge of the tourney field near the goalpost, a plastic trophy between them. He checked the list he and Jane had put together for the quest, and wondered how much longer it would take for the teams to arrive. He was starting to get a little hungry.

"Don't worry, they'll be here soon. It's not an impossible quest," said Jane with a reassuring smile.

They had spent months talking to all the respective parties, negotiating use of locations, and making sure everyone was in on the joke, while keeping things secret from the school administration. Jane had sent long letters to every prince and princess in the kingdom, begging them for access to their treasures, reminding them of their own glory years at Auradon Prep, while Carlos had been the one to keep track of the number of teams playing and make sure that there were enough objects for everyone to collect.

He looked down at the list again:

Collect a shard from Cinderella's glass slipper.
Pluck a flower from Aurora's rose garden.
Cut off a lock of Rapunzel's hair.
Steal a banana from Terk.
Bring back one of Rajah's collars. (Jasmine's tiger had quite a collection.)
Pick an apple from Snow White's orchard.
Take a slice of birthday cake from Mad Hatter's tea party.
Grab a thingamabob from Ariel's collection.
Bake a beignet using Princess Tiana's recipe.
Kiss a prince.
Hum "Be Our Guest" when you get to the finish line.

"I think I hear something. They're here!" said Jane excitedly. She stood up and craned her neck.

Mal and Ben burst out of Ben's carriage. Mal was holding up a fork while Ben was balancing a plate of beignets in one hand and carrying his backpack in the other. The two of them were humming loudly to the tune of "Be Our Guest."

At the same time, Evie and Doug raced to the goalpost from the other side. Evie was holding up a rose while Doug held a satchel of scavenger-hunt objects. They were humming just as loudly, with Evie occasionally bursting into giggles.

It looked like first place would come down to these two teams, but at the last minute, Jay and Lonnie burst from the hedges. Lonnie was carrying a basket with all the items on the list, apples and bananas piled high on top.

All the teams reached the goal line at the same moment, and Mal noticed Evie and Lonnie bolting toward Ben, which reminded her that she too needed to fulfill the second-to-last item in front of the judges: Kiss a prince. All three girls hurriedly leaned in to kiss Ben on the cheek almost at the same time. Almost, that is, because Mal kissed him first. "We win!" said Mal, cheering. "Yay, us!"

Carlos shook his head. "Nope, you all lose."

"What?" they chorused. Mal did a double take, Evie looked affronted, and Lonnie frowned and looked as if she were about to go into battle.

But Jane only laughed and motioned to Chad, who was right behind them. Chad was kissing his own hand. "DONE!" he crowed.

"Ben is a king," said Jane. "The quest is to kiss a *prince*. And well, Chad is kissing a prince, all right."

The group groaned in unison, and Carlos handed Chad the trophy and the gift certificate. "Try the gray stuff. It's delicious," he joked.

"I don't think they serve that at Ariel's Grotto," said Jane. "I think that's Mrs. Potts's recipe."

"Oh, right," said Carlos. "Congratulations, Chad!"

Chad screamed in delight and danced around the goal-posts, hoisting the trophy up in the air as they all looked on with amusement. The rest of the teams arrived, singing and showing each other the treasures they'd scored.

"Congratulations, everyone!" said Jane. "You are all winners!"

"Midnight eats from Snow White's Snack Shack?" Carlos suggested, as his stomach was growling now.

A cheer went up from the crowd of seniors, and they all piled back into their carriages, laughing and high-fiving as they went.

Over the late-night meal, they relived the highlights of the quest. Evie and Doug showed off the scratches on their arms from the thorns from the rose garden, while Jay and Lonnie laughed about how loudly Jay screamed when Rajah caught him sneaking away with one of the tiger's jeweled collars.

When the laughter died down and the crowd at Snow White's trendy new restaurant began to disperse, Mal cleared her throat and leaned in toward her friends. "So, the Royal Council said we can go back to the Isle of the

Lost next weekend to talk to the kids there. Sound good to everyone?"

"Oh! Wonderful!" said Evie.

"Back to the Isle? For sure!" said Jay, who was always up for an adventure.

Only Carlos looked hesitant.

"Carlos?" asked Mal.

"In," he said with a nervous smile. "Always."

"It'll be okay," said Evie, placing an arm around his shoulder. "This is just what you wanted—for everyone to hang out and make the most of our time together."

"Right, thanks for reminding me," said Carlos.

Jane looked a bit worried, but he squeezed her hand. "It'll be all right," he said. "Maybe my mom will be at the spa."

"By the way, it was the best Senior Quest yet! Thanks, you guys, for putting that together," said Evie to Carlos and Jane.

"Wait till you see what we have prepped for graduation!" said Jane.

"We have something planned for graduation?" asked Carlos.

"You'll see!" said Jane.

Carlos beamed. Jane was the best. And, actually, her birthday was coming up in a few months. . . . He'd organize something! She was always doing nice things for everyone else, and he wanted to do the same for her. He'd think of something special—he knew he would.

chapter

12

Where There's Smoke, There's Fire

*Y*es, that was definitely rock music coming from under the depths of the sea. Loud, angry rock music. Uma swam closer to the sound. She recognized it. There was only one resident of the Isle of the Lost who liked playing music at those ear-shattering decibels.

She swam around, looking for the source. But all she could see was gray rock, furry with algae and coral. She swam the length of the rock, where the sound was loudest. *There*. She found a crack, just the smallest crevice. She swam closer. If she could squeeze herself through it, she would be able to get back inside the island. Underground, of course, but still—back on the Isle of the Lost!

Well, she considered, if she could make herself large, she could probably also make herself small. With that, Uma transformed into a tiny squid and slipped through the crack.

When she was back to her human self, she looked around, realizing she was standing on her own two feet once more. It was good to be on dry land again. She was in a tunnel of some sort, an abandoned mine shaft. There were tracks leading deeper underground, where the music was even louder.

Uma followed the tracks all the way down.

All of a sudden, the music was interrupted by the voice of a news anchor from Auradon News Network. "There's been a formal announcement from the palace. As part of her itinerary around the kingdom, the future Lady Mal will be going on an official visit to the Isle of the Lost."

Lady Mal.

Hmpf.

Uma kept walking, her rage growing stronger within her, a plan forming in her head. And then she snuck into his little cave, where the god of the Underworld preferred to spend his days now that he was a prisoner on the Isle of the Lost.

Hades was playing air guitar, pretending he was performing in front of thousands of screaming souls. Or fans. Whatever you wanted to call them.

Uma tapped him on the shoulder and cleared her throat.

Hades jumped and almost hit his head on the cave

ceiling. "Oh! You! What are you doing here? And what's your name again?"

"Uma!"

"Uma? Why did I think it was Shrimpy?" he asked, confused.

She frowned at the reviled nickname. No one called her Shrimpy. *No one.* It made her furious at Mal all over again.

"Hades. You still have that ember of yours, right?"

chapter

13

Pro Tip

The night after the Senior Quest, Lonnie suggested that she and Jay go see one of the professional R.O.A.R. games at the Auradon Arena. Her home team, the Great Wall, was fighting against the Summerland Sevens.

Once they arrived at the stadium, they made their way to a private suite that belonged to Coach Yao, one of the Great Wall's team owners, where a full buffet was laid out. It was complete with burbling chocolate fountains and towering ice sculptures in the likeness of the Great Wall's best player, Lonnie's brother, Li'l Shang. Li'l Shang used to coach R.O.A.R. at Auradon Prep, but had turned pro a few weeks ago.

"Great seats," said Jay, as they filled their plates with an array of delicacies.

"Thanks," said Lonnie with a wink. "I know the owner."

Today's game was tournament-style, which meant pairs of fencers squared off, and whichever team won the most matches won the tournament. The arena showed several matches at the same time. The Summerland Sevens had taken an early lead, with Happy's eldest son, Hap, scoring the most points by the break. The ferocious dwarf had defeated one of the best imperial players. The Summerland Sevens had the advantage of being physically much smaller than the Great Wall team, which meant there were fewer places to hit them at swordpoint.

But Li'l Shang was up next, against Doug's brother Derek. Derek was a hulk of a dwarf, with rippling muscles underneath his R.O.A.R. uniform. He came out swinging, slashing his sword to and fro and racking up points quickly. But Li'l Shang came rushing back, and soon didn't let Derek score another point.

Jay and Lonnie stood and cheered. Jay was so excited he threw his popcorn everywhere. He admired both teams' grit and finesse. Watching Li'l Shang take a flying leap off the edge of the arena to win the match point was positively thrilling.

The players came to the owner's suite after the game, and Li'l Shang grinned when he saw his younger sister and his protégé. "I hoped you guys would be here! What's been going on? How's Auradon Prep?"

"Great! We lost the Kingdom Cup, but we came really close," said Jay, referring to the championship R.O.A.R. game the Auradon Prep team had played several weeks before. "How's life on the pro circuit?"

"Can't complain," said Li'l Shang. "We travel by first-class carriage all the way. Thousands of fans screaming in packed arenas." He pulled open his R.O.A.R. jacket to show Jay a T-shirt with his face on it, SHANG LIFE written in huge letters on the front. "Look! I'm famous!"

Jay laughed. "Dude, you made it!"

"Been trying to get my sister here to join the team, but she says she still hasn't made up her mind whether to go pro or go to college." Li'l Shang rubbed Lonnie's head. "Suit yourself, sis."

Li'l Shang and Lonnie introduced Jay to Coach Yao, who had been a soldier in Mulan's army, along with his partners, Ling and Chien-Po.

"Jay, son of Jafar, of course! I've heard you're one of the best at R.O.A.R.!" he said, shaking Jay's hand. "Ever think of going straight to the pros?"

"Skipping college?" asked Jay.

Yao nodded. "You could be playing in this arena in a few months!"

"You'll have to sign him first," Lonnie reminded him.

"Right, right," said Coach Yao. "And see your moves. We'll be at Auradon Prep next Saturday. We'll check you out."

"Next Saturday?" asked Jay with a frown.

"Is there a problem?"

Jay scratched his head. "Yeah, I'm pretty sure I have . . . a conflict." He never remembered important dates, but he knew this one.

"Oh," said Coach Yao.

Lonnie frowned. "You do?"

"Yeah, I'm supposed to go back to the Isle of the Lost with Mal, Evie, and Carlos. We're going to try to get more kids to apply to Auradon Prep," he told them sheepishly.

"Do you have to?" asked Lonnie. She took Jay aside. "I mean, if you want to be considered for a pro team, this is the only day they'll come to Auradon Prep. It's kind of a big deal."

Jay thought about it. If he missed the recruiting session, Coach Yao wouldn't see him play, and Jay would be passing up the chance to play professionally. He looked around at the arena. He could just imagine it thundering with a thousand fans calling his name. He could do this. He was one of the best. His future was open.

But he couldn't let his friends down. Time with his friends was precious, and it would be even rarer after graduation. They had to stick together. Plus, he wasn't even sure if he wanted to play professionally; there was still college to consider.

"I don't know," said Jay. "I don't really know what I want to do yet."

Lonnie nodded. "I understand. You'll figure it out." They went back to the party.

"Jay?" asked Coach Yao. "Shall we put you down on our list? Will we see you next Saturday?"

"No, you won't. I'm so sorry, but I have other commitments," said Jay.

"No problem. There's always next year," Coach Yao said. "You've got a lot of time to decide."

Jay smiled. The coach was right. He was no longer trapped on the Isle of the Lost. In a few weeks, he had visiting day to look forward to at Sherwood Forest University; the itinerary included a lot of merrymaking. He had all the time in the world right now, and he wanted to spend a good chunk of it with the friends who helped him become the person he was today.

chapter

14

Trade Secrets

The week flew by, and finally it was time for Mal, Evie, Jay, and Carlos to head back to the Isle of the Lost. Mal and Evie had packed so heavily for their short trip that Ben had to help Lumiere and Cogsworth carry their trunks to the royal limousine.

"You know you're only going for the weekend, right?" he asked, grunting under the weight of one particularly large case. "You're only there for two nights."

"Two nights! Oh my! Thank you for reminding me! I almost forgot my second alternate evening gown!" said Evie, who flew back into her room.

Mal smiled. "I'm sorry. Most of it is Evie's."

Carlos and Jay walked right behind them, each boy holding one small backpack. "I travel light," said Jay.

"No baggage," quipped Carlos with a grin. "At least not anymore."

Mal threw her arms around Ben. "Thanks for doing this. Letting us go back to talk to the kids, I mean."

"Yeah, man, we're so pumped that more kids like us are going to be able to go to Auradon Prep!" said Carlos, bumping fists with Jay.

"I am too," said Ben. He really was glad, although he was still a bit worried about where the new VKs would stay over the summer.

Evie rushed back, wheeling another trunk.

"Wait, these things have wheels?" asked Ben as Lumiere and Cogsworth staggered beside him.

"Yes, if you set them down the right way," said Evie. "How do you think I travel?" She chuckled.

They walked out of the school's front doors and loaded their bags into the car. Evie and the boys said their good-byes to Ben and settled into their seats.

Mal lingered, a wistful smile on her face. "I wonder if there'll be a day when we can bring every villain kid over to Auradon."

"There will be. We just need to take it one step at a time. It's too risky right now, especially with Uma still out there."

"Uma," said Mal with a grimace.

"You take care," he said.

"I will. You too. Are you okay?" she asked, putting a hand on his cheek.

"A little nervous about the NAFFA trade meeting. No one can seem to agree lately! I have so many competing proposals to sort out."

"I know you'll make it work. Say hi to the dwarfs," she said, getting into the car.

Evie popped her head out. "Give them my love!"

"I will," said Ben, waving them off. He stood watching by the entrance until the royal limousine disappeared out of sight.

Just as Ben had predicted, every kingdom represented at the trade council argued that their goods were the most valuable.

"They're diamonds," said Grumpy. "We need to be able to charge top Auradon dollar!"

"Diamonds they might be, but our magic potions from Camelot are far more valuable," argued Merlin.

"Everyone will look withered without our age-defying lotions," Eugene Fitzherbert reminded them. "The sundrop golden flowers only grow in Corona."

"We might not have magic flowers or magic potions or diamonds in the bayou," said Princess Tiana. "But we have the best food, and we should be compensated fairly."

Ben listened to every kingdom's representative make their case, and then he spoke his piece: "Just as Auradon

Prep has become open to taking more students from the Isle of the Lost, Auradon must remain open to trade between all our united kingdoms. Diamonds, potions, lotions, and beignets are equally important. Surely we can find a solution that would satisfy everyone here."

The meeting continued, and eventually, all parties were satisfied by the trade agreement. Grumpy didn't even look that grumpy in the end. Ben began to put his papers back into his folder and a few delegates began to leave the room when Aquata, Ariel's oldest sister, who was representing Atlantica, came up to Ben, rolling her bathtub-like contraption forward. "Can I ask you something?" she said, looking worried and splashing a little.

"Of course, anything for a princess of the sea," said Ben with a charming smile.

"We hear from our people that Uma has been seen underwater. She's out there, free to wreak havoc and do whatever she wants."

Ben brushed his hair off his forehead and nodded. "We are aware and have stepped up security. Genie mentioned seeing something near the Isle of the Lost that looked like it could have been a giant octopus. I'll make sure to send more reinforcements to your area if she's seen there," he said, trying to sound reassuring.

"Thank you," said Aquata, sounding a tad relieved. "It's just, her mother . . . her mother almost destroyed my family."

Ben nodded. "I'll make sure everywhere on Auradon is safe, even underwater."

"We're not safe, not anywhere, as long as there's a villain out there," said Aquata, shuddering. "I heard you were going to let more of those people from the Isle come to Auradon. I hope that's just a terrible rumor. Do say it isn't true!"

"Actually, it is true," said Ben. "We'd like to give more people a chance, especially the children, who are innocent. Everyone deserves a chance to be good, don't you think?"

Aquata frowned, and her cheeks flushed. It was clear she did not agree. "I hope you know what you're doing, for all of our sakes."

Ben kept a diplomatic smile on his face. "My main priority, always, is the safety of everyone in Auradon. Now, if you'll excuse me."

Aquata splashed away in a huff, but Ben let it go. He knew it was an almost impossible task, to bring the people of the Isle and the people of Auradon together to live peacefully once more, but he had to keep trying. He had to unite his kingdom somehow. That's what a king was meant to do.

chapter

15

Two of a Kind

*U*ma and Hades faced each other. She crossed her arms, and Hades crossed his. He glared at her. She glared back. It was like they were looking into a mirror; they were both blue-haired villains with a score to settle against their enemies.

"Did I hear you right? Did you ask me if I still have my ember?" said Hades.

"Yes, or are you deaf from all this loud music?" said Uma. "Your ember. Do you have it or not?"

"Why do you ask?" he said imperiously.

"It could be useful," she said, leaning against the wall

of his cave as if she didn't care a whit whether he still had it or not.

Hades frowned. His blue hair stuck up from his forehead like a rock star's, but he had lines around his eyes. Like Uma's mother, Ursula, he'd been on the Isle of the Lost for more than two decades. Uma thought that Hades's life on the Isle of the Lost was probably not all that different from his former life in the Underworld—there was no sunlight down here either.

"Aren't you tired of living underground?" she asked. "In this damp and dreary cave?"

"Is it any better up there?" he scoffed. "On Auradon?"

"You fool! You know it is! I was there! The place is a fairy-tale land!" she told him. "And we should be part of that fairy tale."

Hades yawned. "I'm more of a myth guy."

"Whatever you are, you're not content here. How could you be?" said Uma. "You used to be a god! Don't you guys live on nectar and honey?"

Hades sniffed. "We do have delicate constitutions. Not that you'd know anything about that, being an octopus."

"Sea witch," corrected Uma.

Hades looked suspicious. "By the way, how did you get in here?"

"There was a crack in the tunnel. A tiny one."

"And you fit through it?"

Uma waggled her eyebrows. "I have my ways."

Hades nodded. "Shape-shifter. I get it. So why are you here? Why aren't you out there with your pirates?"

Uma studied her fingernails, affecting insouciance. "I don't want to let anyone know I'm around until my plan is in motion."

"You've got a plan?"

"I do," she said with a crafty smile.

Hades picked up his real guitar and began to pluck a few discordant notes. "Fine. Tell me."

"We should team up, you and I. Together we could bring down the stupid barrier that holds everyone here. Then we could all be free!"

Hades listened. Then he smiled. Then he grinned. "Bring down the barrier, huh?"

"Yes. And I would finally beat Mal." That's all Uma wanted: to show Mal that she could beat her, that Mal didn't get to win every time. So Mal had won the trident, and Ben's heart, but Uma would have this. She would show her old friend, her forever rival, that Uma would have her revenge. Mal would never forget her name, or who freed the Isle of the Lost: UMA.

"Think about it. Once the barrier is down, you could go anywhere and do anything you wanted!" said Uma.

"You don't say?" said Hades. He played a chord and let it echo around the cave.

"I do say," said Uma. "How long have you been here? Twenty years? And how long were you in the Underworld?

They don't remember you up on Olympus anymore. Hades? He's over. He's *nothing*. That's what they say."

"Is that so?" He waggled his eyebrows in frustration.

"I'm afraid so," said Uma with a faux-sad frown. "No one remembers you. All they talk about is Hercules. I've met his kid, Herkie. He's huge as a bull and even more famous than his father."

Hades threw off his guitar and paced the rocky cave floor. Soon he would overturn the lamp and kick the television set. His bad temper was as predictable as the weather.

"And Zeus, well, he's just having a ball up there on Mount Olympus. Every once in a while he throws down his lightning bolts just to remind everyone who's in charge," said Uma. At this point she was completely spitballing. She had no clue what they were doing on Mount Olympus. But Hades didn't have to know that.

"But *I'm* the boss!" cried Hades. "ME!"

"Then help me. Show them," said Uma. "Show them who's boss!"

"I will!" he said, his eyes lighting up. But Uma thought she saw something else flickering there, until he went on, "I'll go back to ruling the world and causing destruction. We must take down the barrier and escape from the Isle of the Lost!"

"Now you're talking," said Uma. She held out her hand. "You know, you're not too bad for a has-been."

Hades cackled. "You ain't seen nothing yet!"

Some Time Ago . . .

Hole in the Sky

Hades paced on the beach and considered his situation. He was not without options. He had to try *something*. He couldn't just rot on this island forever. Come on, were they kidding? He was the lord of the Underworld, the god of the dead! In Olympus, they would be laughing if they saw him looking like some washed-up little minion. Yesterday he'd been offered the most disgusting stew, made by some deluded she-octopus at some little shack. And yet he had forced himself to choke it down, because he was hungry. He had no choice. But he vowed he would not spend one more day on this gods-forsaken rock.

He had an idea.

If there was an invisible barrier around the island, there had to be an end to it, right? It couldn't go on forever, could it? While there were rumors it was a dome, it seemed like it was basically a fence, which meant that he just had to find the top so he could jump over it into freedom! And if it was a dome, maybe the top would be weaker somehow—since the air was thinner up there and maybe the magic was too.

He had corralled a bunch of pirates and promised them treasure chests full of gold if they helped him. Once they were convinced, he had ordered them to build a ladder using some old ships' masts tied together with rope and assorted pieces of wood they found in junk piles. Somehow, they made it work.

The ladder was so long it went almost the entire length of the beach. All they had to do now was set it upright. Then Hades would climb it all the way to the top, punch a hole in the dome with his little invention that he was carrying in a bag strapped across his chest, scale the barrier, and then slide down. He was a god. *Immortal.* Even if he fell from a great height he'd survive. Probably.

"On my count!" he told the crew.

"One, two . . . THREE!"

They heaved the ladder upright. Hades was delighted. "That's what I'm talking about! Now hold it still."

And then he began to climb.

He got dizzy and tried not to look down.

He kept climbing.

He saw mountain peaks in the distance. He spied ravens' nests in their crags. At one point he was so high up that his throat began to tighten from lack of oxygen until he remembered—duh, he was a god. He kept climbing.

He felt like he was practically as high as Olympus! Could he see it from here? Should he call out for Zeus or Athena? Nah, he'd give them a nice surprise when he was on the other side and had all his powers back.

Finally, he reached the end of the ladder. The pirates down below were just a bunch of dots. Hades removed a transistor radio from Jafar's junk shop that he'd been tinkering with; he'd carried it all the way up in his bag. He had this idea to shoot a bolt of electricity at the invisible barrier, sort of like using Zeus's bolts of lightning.

He pressed a switch and sent a huge jet of power blasting at the top of the invisible dome. The dome was supposed to shatter and fall, and everyone would be free. Including Hades!

But nothing happened. It didn't work.

The barrier was still there.

Hades raged. He screamed. He turned red—everywhere but his electric-blue hair, that is. If there had been magic on this side of the barrier, he would have burst into flame.

But instead, in his rage, he just fell off the ladder, back onto the island, hitting the ground with a *thump*.

The pirates looked over. "You all right, dude?"

"I'm alive! I'm alive!" he said. (After all, he'd never been dead.)

Hades picked himself up and looked at the deep crater he'd created. Hmmm. Maybe he was going the wrong way. Maybe he should have been digging instead of climbing all along. . . .

"Pirates!" he called. "I've got a new idea."

No
Place
Like
Home

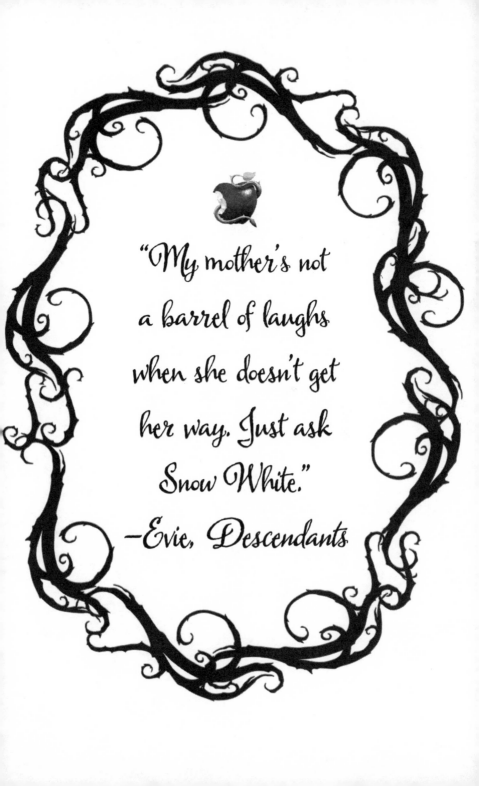

"My mother's not a barrel of laughs when she doesn't get her way. Just ask Snow White."

—Evie, Descendants

chapter

16

Isle Alumni

One thing you could say about the Isle of the Lost was that it never changed. Mal wasn't sure if she loved or loathed that about the place. When Mal, Evie, Carlos, and Jay arrived in the middle of the busy market, everything was exactly as they remembered it. The decrepit tenement buildings covered with peeling paint and graffiti on the sides, the lines of wet, ragged laundry that criss-crossed the plaza, the tin sheds, the hay carts, the vendors hawking everything from holey scarves to varnished trinkets. The sky was gloomy, and everyone looked filthy and sad. This was where they had come from, the neglected island prison where villains were trapped for their crimes against the people of Auradon.

Granted, the four of them had returned to the Isle not so long ago to fetch Mal and then rescue Ben from Uma's clutches. But, just the same, it was still a shock to see it.

Mal glanced up at her mother's old balcony. Her entire childhood had been spent in those shabby rooms above the Bargain Castle that sold wizard robes half price. She used to sit on that balcony and look wistfully over at the mainland, wondering when her life would change. Sometimes Jay came to join her and they would split a bag of stale cheese puffs, their fingers turning as orange as the sunset.

"Come on," said Evie, taking Mal by the arm. "Let's go to our old hideout."

"Hideout?" asked Carlos. "Isn't this an official visit from the palace? Don't we have any other place to stay?"

Evie smiled at him indulgently. "You're cute."

"You'd rather go to your house?" teased Mal.

"Never," said Carlos. "Lead the way."

"There aren't any five-star castles on the Isle of the Lost," Jay chided.

"I just remembered that," said Carlos, smacking his forehead. "If anyone asks, I didn't pack my spa bathrobe, okay?"

A few curious onlookers spotted them in the crowd, but most left them alone. Mal's fearsome reputation tended to keep people away. But even though it seemed like people still feared her, she wondered if they would ever look up to her as a true leader, someone to follow and admire and respect, especially now that she was on official business from Auradon. She tried smiling magnanimously at a street urchin who scurried past them, but the kid just squealed and sped up. Mal sighed. This wasn't going to be easy.

Once they arrived, Carlos found the hidden latch, and Jay threw his shoe at it. The iron door opened, and they walked up to the loft. It was just as they'd remembered, with graffiti on the walls, lumpy mattresses, and trash everywhere.

"Home, sweet hideout," said Evie, wrinkling her nose. Mal knew she was thinking of their pretty room back at school, with its comfortable beds, fat fluffy pillows, neat rows of bookshelves, and lush carpeting. Carlos grimaced at the sight, and Jay looked just as bummed. It was seriously grimy. There was soot on the windowsill, and there were streaks of dirt on the floor.

"It's only for a few days," said Mal, trying to sound comforting.

"I know, I just . . . I always forget what it was like," said Evie.

"Who wants to remember?" Jay smiled. "Dibs on the couch."

Carlos accidentally kicked a trash can, overturning its contents, and one of Harry's hooks rolled out. "Pirates were here. Ugh. No wonder this place is such a dump," he said, his frown deepening.

Jay glared at the mustaches and assorted doodles the

pirates had drawn on the portraits of the four of them that Mal had painted on the walls. "Animals!" he pronounced, and went to look for a rag.

They made the place as habitable as they could, sweeping up the trash and scrubbing the floors. Evie put clean sheets on the beds and unpacked the pillows she'd brought from Auradon. "Thank goodness you don't travel light," said Carlos, looking relieved.

"Never," promised Evie, removing a vase and flowers from the bottom of her trunk. She looked around at the newly clean and brightened space. They had brought a little Auradon to their old pad. "Better."

"Let's get going," said Mal. She felt a rush of energy. "I want to make the announcement as soon as possible."

They left and locked the hideout, and Mal led them out through the crowded bazaar back to her old castle. Inside, everything was covered with a thick layer of dust, from Maleficent's old throne to the green refrigerator that still held goblin slime from two years ago. For a moment, Mal felt sad about her mother, who was still trapped as a lizard—wherever she was now.

Mal braced herself to go out on the balcony and address the crowd.

"Hold on," said Evie, brushing Mal's hair from her forehead and pulling up her jacket collar. "Better."

"Thanks," said Mal, trying not to feel too nervous.

"You've got this, okay? It's a great plan, and I know you're going to do Auradon proud," reassured Evie.

"I just really want this to work," said Mal, taking a deep breath.

"I know. Me too," said Evie.

"You're gonna be great!" said Carlos. Jay grinned and clapped Mal on the shoulder for encouragement. She smiled and stepped onto the balcony.

Mal took her place and raised her hands to signal for attention. Jay, Carlos, and Evie walked behind her, fanning out so that everyone could see them. Mal hoped they looked like a power squad, and not like a bunch of kids who didn't know what they were getting themselves into.

A hush fell over the crowd as the people of the Isle of the Lost spotted them. But whatever Mal had expected their reaction to be, it wasn't this. The audience shrank back, whispering wildly and gesturing with fright toward the four of them. Some people even seemed to be trembling! A few of the little ones were outright crying. Mal looked around in confusion and disbelief. She knew she had a reputation, but how scary did they really think she was?

Evie crept up beside her. "Um . . . Mal?"

Mal stage-whispered back, "What's going on? Why do they look so freaked-out?"

Carlos cleared his throat. "Well, we're kind of standing in the shadows," he said, gesturing to the overhang that was cloaking them in darkness. "I think that they think you're, well, your mom."

It was only then that Mal could make out the fervent, terrified whispers from the crowd. "Maleficent!" they were saying. "She's back!" Someone in the crowd shrieked and ran away.

Mal tugged down the collar of her jacket—which might have looked a bit cape-like in silhouette, she realized. But, come on, it's not like she had *horns*. She stepped out of the shadows and into the sunlight.

"Guys, guys," she said, waving her hands. "It's me, Mal!" *And my mom is like, eating leaves and lying on a rock somewhere*, she wanted to add, but didn't.

A murmur rippled through the crowd as terror turned into something that resembled relief, but a relief that was definitely still tinged with terror. *Mal! She's back! Mal's going to curse us! Why is she here? Who's that behind her? Why, it's the four of them! They're all back! I like Evie's dress! What's Mal going to do to us?!*

"I hope my mother doesn't find out I'm here," muttered Carlos, standing next to Evie.

"Shhh," said Evie, who was waving to the crowd and blowing kisses like a true princess. "Everyone calm down! We have good news!" called Evie, but the crowd ignored her and continued to churn with nervous energy.

Jay stepped forward. "Settle down, settle down!" he commanded. "Go on, Mal, tell them."

Mal raised her hands once more for silence. This time, she got it.

"Hi," she started again, then took a breath and squared her shoulders. "I have an official announcement from the kingdom of Auradon. Auradon Prep is taking more applications from the Isle of the Lost!" Mal paused, glancing around for applause or gasps of excitement. But they were only staring up at her silently. "Four new kids are going to be selected to attend the school, just like we were. I promise you, this is the opportunity of a lifetime, and I hope you'll all consider applying. Join us on the mainland!"

Mal finished her announcement with a grin and waited. But the villains were just shaking their heads. They grumbled to each other: *School? Who wants to go to school? Auradon? Why would we want to go there? This is stupid. Homework? Ew.*

The crowd began to disperse, muttering and shaking their heads. Evie rushed up next to Mal, her arms outstretched. "Wait! Hear us out! Please!"

"Please?" Mal heard one of the kids scoff. No one ever used common courtesies like *please* on the Isle. Mal thought that most of them must have been shocked into complying, though, because they all seemed to pause.

"Yes, listen!" said Carlos. "We've had a great time in Auradon! There are so many delicious things to eat that aren't even rotten or expired. And so many awesome desserts!"

"There's this game called tourney," said Jay. "Where you can really beat someone up!" Evie shot him a look and he shrugged. "You have to give them what they want to hear."

Mal nodded. Jay was right. They would never be able to explain the appeal of Auradon to people who only knew life on the Isle of the Lost. But she had to try.

"I was like you once," she said. "I just wanted to live a wicked life, full of treachery and evil deeds. But Auradon changed me. I realized there's more to life than being wicked."

"Like what?" sneered a snaggletoothed witch.

"Well . . ." said Mal, searching for something the crowd would respond to. "There's strawberries—these amazing fruits that burst with flavor on your tongue!"

"And there's this stuff called peanut butter!" said Carlos. "It's . . . like butter! Made from peanuts!"

"They don't know what butter is except that it's rancid," Evie reminded him in a whisper. "Let me try." She stepped up to the railing. "Like Mal said, there's more to life than being evil. There's loyalty and friendship." The four of them linked hands and smiled at each other.

"You will find friends who will do anything for you," said Carlos.

"You'll discover that you're more than what you thought you were," added Jay, and they lifted their hands to the sky in unison.

"And there's love," said Mal, feeling tears come to her

eyes. She was Maleficent's daughter, born and bred to hate, to plot, to scheme, to command minions to do her bidding. Mistress of Darkness. Queen of the Isle of the Lost. But all she felt for this ragged, unruly crowd was deep empathy and affection. Mal wished they could all understand that there were greater things to live for than revenge or violence or pettiness, greed, and graft.

The crowd still didn't look too convinced, but Mal thought it was a good start. She had to give them time. Even the four of them took a while to discover they were better off in Auradon than the Isle of the Lost.

chapter

17

Big, Bad Voodoo Daddy

The next morning, they all headed back to their old stomping grounds at Dragon Hall. Evie felt a momentary rush of nostalgia for the place. Even though it was no Auradon Prep, she had always loved coming to Dragon Hall—especially after all those isolated years of castle-schooling. The front steps of the mausoleum were full of students tripping each other and pushing their way up the stairs in the usual morning chaos. Once again, the kids stared as they noticed Mal, Jay, Carlos, and Evie in their midst.

The whispers buzzed through the crowd. *Isn't that Mal?*

What's she doing here? Did you hear she turned her mother into a lizard? Don't stare or she'll turn you into one!

Evie saw that Mal was trying to smile at them, but when she did, the kids ran from her. "How am I ever going to connect with them if they can't see past my old reputation?" she asked Evie with a sigh. "I'm not my mom. It seems like people in Auradon finally get that. But maybe everyone on the Isle will always think of me as the old Mal."

"They'll come around," Evie said firmly, as she looped her arm through Mal's.

"And if they don't, Mal will burn them with her dragon fire," said Jay with a laugh.

The girls glared at him. "Not the point, Jay," said Mal.

He held up his hands in surrender. "I was just kidding!"

A trembling LeFou Deux awaited them at the entrance of the school. "Welcome back to Dragon Hall. Please follow me. Dr. Facilier is expecting you." He groveled, bowing so low his forehead almost touched the floor.

LeFou Deux led them to the headmaster's hidden office in the Athenaeum of Secrets. Dr. Facilier was seated at his faded velvet chair, but he stood when they entered. "Welcome back," he said with a terrifying grin. He was as tall and slender as ever—almost as thin as his mustache. He shook their hands with his long, bony fingers. Dr. Facilier never failed to strike fear into the hearts of Dragon Hall's pupils, and Evie knew the four of them were having difficulty remembering that they were no longer under his supervision. They were Auradon Prep students now, and protected by Fairy Godmother, she reminded herself.

"Now, what brings the four of you here?" he asked as they all sat down. "Not looking to come back, I presume? Or are you?" He laughed heartily at his own joke.

Evie shot the other three a nervous smile. "Planning to trap us here, Dr. Facilier?" she asked lightly.

"Oh, no, no," he said, with a wave of his hand. "As much as I would enjoy trying, I don't think that would be beneficial to anyone."

Mal cleared her throat and sat up straight. "Auradon Prep is expanding its program to bring more students from the Isle of the Lost over to the mainland," she told him. "So we were hoping you could distribute these applications and encourage kids to sign up. And as you discussed with the Royal Council, tomorrow we will be available to talk to students and answer any questions they might have about Auradon."

Carlos opened his backpack and handed over a stack of papers to their old headmaster. "Here you go," he said.

Dr. Facilier picked up one of the documents. "And how many kids from the Isle of the Lost is Auradon Prep accepting?"

"Four," said Jay.

"I see," Dr. Facilier said, as he continued to study the forms. "And if I do this for you, what's my cut?"

Mal blinked. "Your cut?"

"Excuse me?" asked Evie, as Carlos hesitated to remove more application forms from his backpack.

"Your cut," said Jay, deadpan. "Your bribe, you mean."

The headmaster of Dragon Hall leaned back on his chair, put his feet up on his desk, and took a moment to admire his shiny shoes. "Exactly. What do I get in return for sending students to your program?"

"The joy of knowing they're learning and well cared for!" Evie said indignantly.

"Dr. Facilier, that's not really how it works," said Mal sharply. "We don't do kickbacks or deliver bribes. Especially not in Auradon."

Dr. Facilier chuckled, sending shivers up their spines. "Let me remind you, you're back on the Isle of the Lost now."

"What do you want?" Jay asked bluntly.

"Yeah, spill it," said Carlos.

Evie looked at the boys, alarmed, but Mal nodded. "I suppose it's the price of doing business," she said. Mal gave Evie a look that said, *Just trust me.*

"I'm glad we're in agreement," said Dr. Facilier with a smug smile. "I don't ask for much. You know my younger daughter Celia, don't you?"

Mal narrowed her eyes. "I don't think we've met, no."

"She feels very left out when she hears all the stories that her sister Freddie has been telling her about Auradon. Very left out indeed," said Dr. Facilier meaningfully.

Mal and Evie exchanged a glance. "We're not on the admissions committee," said Evie.

"But I'm sure you could put in a good word," said Dr. Facilier.

Mal raised an eyebrow. "We'll take that under advisement," she said. "That is, if you honor your end of the bargain."

"You see that you do," said Dr. Facilier. "So, for tomorrow, you will be speaking with students at some kind of roundtable discussion?"

"Yes," said Mal. "We're going to tell them all about Auradon Prep! I believe we've been given the study hall for our presentation."

Dr. Facilier sighed. "Fine, I don't see how I can stop you, since I've been ordered by Fairy Godmother to let you in."

Mal nodded. The four of them began to stand up to say their good-byes.

"Also," said Evie, "we're going to be sending over posters—marketing materials, to encourage the kids to apply. It would be great if we could put up some here at Dragon Hall as well."

Dr. Facilier shrugged. "I suppose we could agree to that," he said.

"Great," said Mal.

"Just remember her name: Celia."

"Of course," said Mal. "We'll do our best."

The four of them shook Dr. Facilier's hand. Evie knew

they weren't in the business of taking bribes; if Celia deserved to get in to Auradon Prep, she would. But it would be on her own merit, not because the VKs swayed the committee. They left the application forms at the headmaster's office and reminded him of the deadline.

"A pleasure doing business with you," said Dr. Facilier, ushering them out of his office. "Oh, and here's Celia now. Celia, come meet these fine folk."

Celia jumped back. It was obvious to Evie that she had been eavesdropping at the door. "Oh! Hi, Dad," she said. She wore a red dress and a little top hat that matched her father's, and she was holding a deck of cards.

"Celia, this is Mal, Evie, Carlos, and Jay. They used to be my top students here, but unfortunately they go to Auradon Prep now."

"Nice to meet you," said Celia. "Want to hear your fortune?"

Dr. Facilier smiled proudly. "That's my girl." He closed the door, and the four VKs were left in the hallway with Celia.

They all hesitated, but it was clear Celia was intent on reading someone their cards.

"Sure, tell me my fortune," Evie relented. She could humor the kid, right?

"We're going to talk to a few more teachers to make sure they tell kids about the Auradon Prep roundtable tomorrow," said Mal. "I don't trust Dr. Facilier to get those applications out. Maybe Lady Tremaine can help, since Dizzy really wants to go to Auradon."

"Sounds like a plan," said Carlos. "Jay, you go find Coach Gaston in PE, and I'll hit up Madam Mim."

"I'll go meet Professor Gothel and catch up with you guys at the hideout after hearing my fortune," said Evie.

They nodded and went their separate ways.

Celia led Evie to a quiet desk in the library. She offered the cards to Evie to shuffle. Evie closed her eyes and shuffled them. Celia took the cards back and laid them out in three piles. Then she revealed the top card of each deck. "These three cards represent the past, the present, and the future," she told Evie. "The first card is the Tower. It means you came from a difficult past. You were trapped and in danger."

"Pretty much. I mean, I am from the Isle of the Lost," said Evie. "I was exiled to our castle with my mother, the Evil Queen."

"Dangerous indeed," said Celia.

"When I missed our usual Friday face mask, she wanted to murder me," said Evie with a roll of her eyes. In truth, she did miss her shallow, beauty-obsessed mother just a little bit. Still, she would rather keep her distance while they were on the Isle; it just wasn't worth it when her mother would never understand the things Evie wanted to accomplish. "On Thursdays we practiced smiling and waving."

Celia snorted. She pointed to the second card on the

table. "The Ten of Pentacles. This is your present. It means you have strength behind you. That you belong to a group of people who have your back. They bring you a lot of luck."

Evie smiled. "I have an amazing group of friends."

"And the third card is your future. Oh," said Celia staring at the card. "It's dark."

"It is?" asked Evie nervously.

"Very. This is the Judgment card. It means change, mostly for the worse. This card means disaster is on the horizon. Something terrible is about to happen. Aaaaaaand"—Celia drew out the word, quirking her eyebrows at Evie—"if you want to know how to prevent it, you'll have to buy another session."

"Another session! How much was this one?" asked Evie. "I didn't realize you charged."

"Of course I do. Nothing's free in this world." Celia smirked and named her price.

"Okay," said Evie, opening her purse and handing over a few gold coins. "But I'm not paying for another one."

"Really? I don't advise that. You should really find out how to avoid whatever it is the Judgment has foretold. Or you should at least try to discover who is conspiring against you guys."

Evie knew a hustle when she saw one. "Nice try, but I'll take my chances," she said with a sweet smile.

"Suit yourself," said Celia, putting her cards away.

Evie shook her head. She was far from superstitious and

was highly skeptical that the future could be divined from a few fortune cards. She wondered about Celia's chances with the Auradon Prep admissions committee. So far, all Evie could see was a trickster through and through. But, of course, that didn't mean there wasn't more to Celia— after all, there had been more to Evie and her friends. It was going to be interesting to see if Celia ended up at Auradon, that was for sure.

chapter

18

This Little Light of Mine

The same day that Mal and her friends were meeting with Dr. Facilier at Dragon Hall, Uma returned to Hades's lair. The blue-haired ex–god of the dead was snoring on his couch, a little line of drool dripping from his open mouth. He woke up with a start when Uma cleared her throat.

"You again?" said Hades, rubbing the sleep from his eyes. "I thought we had a deal. You agreed to leave me alone," he groused.

"That wasn't our deal," said Uma, annoyed. "And did you ever think of doing any housekeeping around here? This cave reeks."

Hades looked affronted. "I'm sorry my league of demons are more interested in preying on souls than vacuuming. Anyway, did you hear that Mal was spotted on Maleficent's balcony last night? I thought it might interest you, given our agreement."

Uma looked furious. "She's back on the Isle of the Lost, is she?"

"That's right," said Hades, a strange look on his face. Uma thought she caught something that almost looked like regret there. But regret for what?

"Ugh! I can just picture it. Mal and her little minions, strutting around thinking they're so great, as if they own the place, when all they did was abandon it!" said Uma, who could never stand the way Mal and her friends acted like the Isle was their territory. The Isle of the Lost was *her* turf. She ached to reveal herself to Mal and show them exactly who was the real lady of this island. But she had to stay focused on the plan. If she showed her hand too quickly, she might lose her advantage. She had to be patient. And she had to have Hades on her side.

"Okay, so?" said Hades, who was now looking through his record collection to find something to play on his ancient record player.

Uma raised an eyebrow at the albums Hades picked up. They never got anything good on the Isle, only Auradon castoffs that no one on the island really wanted. *Sebastian the*

Crab's Greatest Hits. Genie Sings the Blues. Eugene Fitzherbert and His Polka Band.

She shook her head impatiently. "So we need to get to Mal. If we can get to Mal, I can get hold of the remote control that opens the barrier. Click—open and out."

"Sounds simple enough," said Hades.

"Except I can't get that close. She knows I'll cause trouble for her, so if she sees me, she'll run the other way. I need her to come to me, where she won't be able to escape."

Hades barked a laugh and gave up searching for a decent record. He grabbed a copy of his own band's last album instead. "She's a smart one to avoid you, then."

"Obviously," said Uma. "But we can't give up just yet. You said you still have your ember, right?"

"Yeah, but I hate to break it to you, kid, it doesn't glow anymore. It's useless." Hades flopped down on one of the broken recliners in his cave and opened an expired canned coffee drink from the Slop Shop. He took a big gulp and grimaced. "Black as my soul indeed."

Uma shook her head. "Do you see all these cracks in the tunnel?" she asked, pointing to the fissures on the cave wall and ceiling.

"Yeah? So what?"

She leaned over so she was almost in his face. "I think these cracks might let in a little magic. We're so far beneath the island that Fairy Godmother's spell is weaker down here."

Hades perked up. "A little magic? Is that so?" He put away his coffee.

"There's only one way to find out, isn't there? Bring it out," she ordered. "Let's see if it still works."

Hades sighed and got up to fetch the ember. "I usually keep it in my sock drawer . . ." he said. "Hmm. When was the last time I had it? Ah, here we go." He strode over to his desk and grabbed it from where it had been holding down a stack of papers.

"It's dead; I was using it as a paperweight," he said, showing it to Uma. In his hand was a gray rock. It was just a hunk of coal, nothing more. No spark.

"Try it," Uma urged.

He waved a hand above it. Nothing happened. He waved his hand once more. Still nothing. "I told you, it's useless. . . ."

"THERE!" yelled Uma.

A minuscule, almost imperceptible spark of blue light shone in the center of the gray stone. It was barely there, but still—it was definitely glowing.

Uma hooted. "I told you!"

Hades gazed at his ember with what looked like love. It wasn't enough magic to get them out of there, but it was magic. He wasn't powerless after all.

"You need Mal to come to you, right?" he asked thoughtfully.

"Right."

"Leave it to me. I'll take care of Mal."

"Perfect. And, Hades? Don't fail me. Or I'll feed you to my mother," Uma threatened with a toss of her turquoise braids.

"That would improve her stew, if you ask me," said Hades. "Now scram!"

chapter

19

The Walls Have Ears

*D*r. Facilier would've been proud to know that, at that very moment, his daughter Celia was cutting class and sneaking around the Isle of the Lost instead of sitting through another boring lecture about the history of evil. After failing to sell Evie on another fortune reading, Celia had snuck out of Dragon Hall through the basement, which led to an underground tunnel system that snaked all around the island. It was an easy way to get around without being seen.

The tunnels were dark and damp, and rumor had it that magic had once run wild down here, creating wondrous lands underneath the island, along with a pathway that led to Auradon itself. That is, until Mal and her friends had shut off the entrance to the Catacombs and the magical barrier was reinforced once more, Celia recalled glumly. Now there was just the one underground channel, through a leftover mine shaft.

Celia was winding through the mine shaft and approaching Hades's cave when she heard a new voice inside with him. Hades hardly ever had visitors. It was why she ran errands for him sometimes. So who was there now? The voice sounded highly annoyed. Celia strained her ears until she recognized it with a start. That could only belong to one surly pirate queen: *Uma*. Uma was back! What were they talking about? Celia tried to press her ear to the wall, but she couldn't make out much. Something about the barrier, it sounded like. "Click—open and out," she heard Uma say, but it was hard to hear the rest.

"I'll take care of Mal," she heard Hades say. There was more murmuring, and then Hades boomed, "Now scram!"

That she heard loud and clear.

The door to the cave opened with a bang, and Celia pressed herself against the tunnel walls, hoping Uma wouldn't see her. But Uma never appeared. She definitely wasn't in Hades's cave anymore, though. After his outburst, Hades's lair had gone silent.

Take care of Mal?

Click—open and out? What was that?

What were Hades and Uma planning?

It had to be an escape of some sort. A way to get off the Isle of the Lost. That was all Uma—and every other villain on the Isle—had ever wanted.

Celia felt her heart beat loudly in her chest. She bolted out of the tunnel and ran all the way back up to Dragon Hall, where she bumped into Dizzy, who was leaving her Introduction to Scheming class. She and Dizzy had become good friends ever since Dizzy had designed her the little hat she wore—at least, as good of friends as anyone could be on the Isle. Celia *loved* her hat. "Dizzy!" she called, trying to push her way through the crowd of villains in the hallway.

"Yes?" asked Dizzy, pushing up her glasses.

Celia looked around the halls to make sure no one was listening. "Want to hear the craziest thing?" She liked being the first to know and share gossip around the Isle.

"Um . . . I guess so?" said Dizzy, looking wary.

"They're going to let four more kids from here go to school in Auradon," said Celia. "Just like Mal and her friends!"

Dizzy yelped in glee. "They are? Do you think they'll finally take me?"

"You were invited. Of course they'll take you! But this

means three more kids will get to come too. Maybe I'll be one of them!" said Celia.

Dizzy squealed. "That would be wicked! Wicked good, you know."

"And I could finally hang out with my older sister Freddie too. She owes me some money from when I read her fortune before she left."

"Oh, Celia," said Dizzy. "You never change."

"I know." Celia drummed her fingers together and smirked. Dizzy gave her a look that said she didn't approve of whatever Celia was scheming. But Celia just laughed. Then she remembered the next part of her news. "Oh, and . . ." She was about to tell Dizzy more, but the second bell rang and Dizzy had to run.

Celia shrugged. Uma and Hades were definitely planning to bring down the barrier somehow and let everyone out. Except, hmm . . . Uma and Hades hadn't succeeded at anything yet, and probably wouldn't succeed at this either. The only thing they would achieve would be getting everyone on the Isle of the Lost in trouble.

And if everyone on the Isle of the Lost was in trouble, then no one would be allowed to go to Auradon. That would definitely cut into her plan of bringing her card-reading gig to Auradon. Not ideal, since they were so very trusting over there.

She began to shuffle her cards like she did when she was

feeling anxious. Was this the bad fortune she always predicted for everyone when she read them their cards?

Should she do something about it? Like warn Mal and her friends, maybe?

Maybe.

chapter
20

Blasts from the Past

*E*verywhere Mal went in Dragon Hall, it was like her old life was mocking her. She had her work cut out for her to convince everyone that she was straight and true, that was for sure. It was hard for them to believe she was really Mal of Auradon now. To them, she would always be Maleficent's rotten little spawn. Or worse, if they did believe she was good, they were disappointed in her. That much was clear when she went to meet with Lady Tremaine, who had once taught her Advanced Evil Schemes. The evil stepmother was less than thrilled to see her best student fall into the "clutches of good," as she put it.

"Oh, Mal, how far you've fallen," sighed Lady Tremaine. "And now you've corrupted my little Dizzy as well."

"I'm proud of Dizzy," said Mal. "She's a great kid."

Lady Tremaine waved her hand dismissively. "I suppose I should rest my hopes on my other grandchildren. I know why you're here."

"You know about the VK program? And the Auradon Prep roundtable tomorrow?"

"Yes, yes, yes, we received the royal proclamation and heard about your . . . shall we say, *ineffective* balcony announcement," said Lady Tremaine, sniffing. She picked up the application form that Mal had placed on her desk and read it out loud: "'Mal and King Ben ask you to be truthful and sincere, and to always speak from the heart.'" The steely-eyed professor looked over at Mal through her pince-nez glasses. "Where on earth do you think you'll find students who will act that way? Not here."

Mal flushed. "We need to find them, to unite our divided kingdom."

"Good luck," said Lady Tremaine drily.

"I know there are students at this very school who have the courage to join us in Auradon. I was one," said Mal. "I just didn't know it back then." She tried to sit straighter and project some kind of authority. Ben always seemed to be able to command the respect of the room in his council meetings. Why couldn't Mal convince just this one person to take her seriously?

Lady Tremaine drummed her fingers on her desk. "The Mal I knew excelled at evil pranks; the Mal I knew spelled a boy to force him to fall in love with her. The Mal I knew is just biding her time to rule the kingdom." She winked. "That *is* what you're doing, isn't it?"

Mal was about to protest when she nodded. If she couldn't beat 'em, she would at least pretend to join 'em. In the end, she just wanted to make sure the kids came to the discussion tomorrow and had access to the applications, even if she and Lady Tremaine couldn't see eye to eye. "Exactly."

"Excellent. I will be happy to find such students to send you tomorrow," said Lady Tremaine.

Coach Gaston was running doomball drills when Jay interrupted to talk about the new VK program. Gaston looked the same as he always did: dark-haired, aggressively handsome with his swell cleft of a chin, and still as large as a barge. "You want me to talk to the kids about going to school in Auradon?" he asked, scratching his incredibly thick neck. "And send them to some event you have planned tomorrow?"

"Would you, Coach?" asked Jay.

Gaston shrugged. "What do they have in Auradon that's so great, anyway?"

"For starters, they can have five dozen eggs for breakfast if they want," said Jay, who knew the way to Gaston's heart was through his breakfasts.

"We have that here," said Gaston. "Rotten, of course, but you get used to the taste."

"Right," Jay said with a sigh. "I'll leave the forms here, just in case."

Madam Mim was in between teaching classes in alchemy when Carlos arrived. "Shut the door!" she screeched when he entered. "You're letting in too much sunlight! Bah! I hate sunlight!"

"Okay! Sorry!" said Carlos. "How are you, Professor?"

"As bad as can be," moaned Madam Mim. "Ever since they closed off the Catacombs I've been terribly hungry." Madam Mim used the old tunnels to poach sheep and wildlife from the farms surrounding Camelot. She had quite a large appetite when she was in her dragon form. She narrowed her eyes suddenly. "Weren't you one of the kids responsible for shutting them down?"

"W-well, um . . ." Carlos stammered. Then he shook his head. His mother might be terrifying, but he wasn't going to let himself be intimidated by Madam Mim. "Sorry about that," he said. "But that's not what I'm here to talk about today."

"Then what's this all about? That Auradon program, is it?" Madam Mim sniffed.

"Yes! Would you mind distributing these forms to your students? And reminding them that four of us from Auradon Prep will be taking questions tomorrow during study hall?" He deliberately didn't call it a *roundtable*, so as not to upset Madam Mim with bad memories of Arthur and his knights.

"I suppose I could," said Madam Mim, taking the stack of papers from him. "Although why anyone would want to stay in Auradon for that long, I don't know. It's always sunny there."

Evie had always been Mother Gothel's favorite student during her time at Dragon Hall; Evie had excelled in her Self-Interest, Selfishness, and Selfies classes. Mother Gothel was trying out another age-defying skin cream when Evie found her in the faculty lounge.

"Evie! Your skin! It's glowing!" said Mother Gothel jealously. "What's your secret?"

"Fresh air, exercise, and a healthy diet," Evie replied with a smile.

"Bah!" said Mother Gothel. "Who wants to do that?"

"Try it, you might like it," said Evie cheerfully. She set a bunch of applications in front of her former professor. "I wanted to drop these off with you, to give to your students. Did you hear about the VK program?"

"Who hasn't?" said Mother Gothel, curling her lip. "You know we're all gossips here on the Isle."

Evie's smile faltered a little. "Well, the four of us are going to be taking any questions tomorrow during a round-table at study hall. If anyone's curious about Auradon Prep, they can come and talk to us. It would be great if you could let people know."

Mother Gothel shrugged. "People make their own decisions around here."

"Please," said Evie. She opened her purse and removed a tiny jar of moisturizer and pushed it across the table. "From me, as a token of my appreciation." If it would help get a few kids to apply to Auradon Prep, was it truly that bad?

Mother Gothel snatched it up greedily without a word of thanks, but, of course, Evie hadn't expected any.

The four friends met back up in the loft at the end of the day. They were hungry for dinner, so Evie opened her trunk again and set out a full meal, pulling out a picnic blanket, a cooler full of icy drinks, and hot containers of fried chicken and mashed potatoes. "Bless you," said Carlos, awed by the incredible spread in front of them. "I thought we'd have to go to Ursula's Fish and Chips Shoppe to eat."

"Or the Slop Shop," said Jay with a shudder. "Goblin cuisine. Blegh. I used to get the worst stomachaches."

"Preparation is the key to success," said Evie, spooning out braised greens and yams.

"And Mrs. Potts," added Mal.

"Hear, hear," agreed Evie, handing out napkins and utensils. They helped themselves and murmured their thanks to the benevolent school cook.

"So how'd it go?" Evie asked. "Do you think we'll get

more applications? And anyone to come to the roundtable tomorrow?"

"We tried," said Mal. "Hopefully."

"Who knows?" said Jay. "They'd be silly to miss out on Auradon Prep."

Carlos shrugged. He was too busy eating.

There was a knock on the secret door, and Evie went to answer it. "Oh, hey, Celia," she said. "What's up? I don't think anyone else is interested in having their fortune read."

"No, I'm not here for that," said Celia, flushing a little.

"Okay," said Evie, ushering her inside. "Come and have a bite to eat with us, then."

Celia's eyes grew wide at the picnic spread. For a moment, the four VKs felt guilty for the bounty they shared. No one ate this well on the island. "Here, have a doughnut," said Carlos.

"Thanks," said Celia, and took a big bite.

"So, what's up?" asked Mal.

Celia put down the doughnut and fidgeted with the sleeve of her dress. "I came to tell you guys: Uma's back. She's definitely on the Isle of the Lost somewhere. And I think she's coming for you, Mal."

Mal wiped her mouth with a napkin. "Uma hasn't been seen anywhere, Celia," she said reassuringly. "I promise, Ben and I have been taking the security of both Auradon and the Isle very seriously. Anyway, if she were back, she'd be with her pirates."

"But my cards foretell doom and disaster," said Celia.

Jay cocked his eyebrow. "Do they, now?"

"I wouldn't believe everything the cards say," said Evie, shaking her head and starting to put things away, folding up the picnic blanket and saving the leftovers in plastic containers.

"Whatever it is, we can take care of it," said Carlos. "Don't worry about us."

"But I heard Uma's voice! And we all know Uma is *dangerous*," said Celia defensively. "She already attacked you guys once!"

"We're leaving the day after tomorrow," said Mal. "We'll be fine. And we will watch out for Uma, I promise." But Evie saw something flicker in Mal's eyes. Was Mal worried? Were they safe from Uma? Evie shook away her thoughts. Everything was fine. They were just here to do a job. Nothing bad was going to happen!

"Okay," said Celia finally. "Don't say I didn't warn you."

"We won't," said Mal. "Thanks for coming by."

"If something happens, you owe me for predicting it correctly," said Celia with a smirk. "I take gold coins. Lots of them."

"How can we forget?" said Jay drily.

They said good-bye to Celia, and Evie sent her off with the leftovers. Mal locked the door behind her.

"Do you really think Uma's back on the Isle?" asked Carlos, when it was just the four of them.

"Anything's possible," said Mal. "We'll keep watch."

"Okay, I'll take the first shift," said Jay.

"Uma again," said Evie with a sigh. She supposed that, on an island full of villains, they should be glad there was only one to worry about, but it was a fitful night's sleep nevertheless.

chapter
21

Square Pegs in a Round Table

When he lived on the Isle, Jay used to sleep in until noon, but now that he was an Auradon kid, he was up bright and early the next day—even if he had been up all night keeping watch for anything suspicious. There was too much to do to stay in bed! The four of them had to get ready for the roundtable event they'd planned for study hall. "Do you think anyone will show?" asked Carlos, yawning as they made their way back to campus.

"I hope so," said Evie, looking determined. She had made a slideshow and everything, even giving it a sound track.

"They will," said Mal. "If only out of curiosity."

"Curiosity killed the cat," Jay reminded them with a grin. "But in this case, curiosity will send people to Auradon!"

When they arrived, they discovered to their dismay that the room used for study hall was covered in dust and cobwebs, and it made Jay sneeze. "We forgot," said Evie. "No one actually *goes* to study hall."

"Because no one studies," said Carlos. "It's Dragon Hall."

They set about clearing the cobwebs and putting the chairs in a semicircle. Then they waited for students to arrive. Minutes ticked by. Mal fiddled with her notes. Evie took out her journal and sketched some dresses. Carlos did homework. Jay paced the room, unable to keep still.

"You guys, I don't think anyone is coming," he said.

"Maybe we should have met with Yen Sid? You know, and his secret Anti-Heroes Club?" said Evie. "They were helpful in shutting down the Catacombs that time, remember?"

"Yen Sid is on a sabbatical. He's actually back in Auradon—I checked yesterday after meeting with Coach Gaston," said Jay. "And the Anti-Heroes Club was disbanded by Dr. Facilier when he found out it was actually a pro-heroes and anti-villains club. I think those kids are a bit freaked-out."

"Bummer," said Carlos. "They would have been great candidates."

"Shhh," said Mal. "I think someone's here."

The door creaked open. Ginny Gothel, who used to be one of Mal's friends on the island, entered. "I think I'm in the wrong place. This isn't the world-domination seminar, is it?" she asked.

"No!" said Mal. "But it could be. I mean, you could learn about how to dominate the world for good."

"Why would I want to do that?" sneered Ginny with a toss of her curly black hair.

"It would mean getting out of here," said Jay. "For one."

Ginny thought it over and took a seat. "Okay."

Jay shot Mal a triumphant grin. Mal grinned back.

"We're going to wait for a few more students before we get started," said Mal.

Jay hoped there would be a few more, but he wasn't counting on it. Then the door opened again, and Anthony Tremaine walked inside. Anastasia's son was as fastidiously dressed as ever; even though his jeans were patched, they were still immaculate. He raised an eyebrow when he saw Jay. "Oh, it's you," he said in a haughty voice.

"You," Jay said with a menacing tone. Then he smiled happily. "I was hoping I'd run into you! Here you go." He handed Anthony his wallet. "I've been holding on to it for a while, I stole it a long time ago. Sorry."

Anthony took it back with a dubious look on his face. He opened the wallet and counted the bills inside.

"It's all in there," said Jay.

"*Quelle suprise*," said Anthony, who liked to make people feel inferior by speaking in French. "My grandmother sent me."

He sullenly took a seat next to Ginny Gothel, just as LeFou Deux walked in. The squat little boy looked nervously at the older kids in the room. "Coach Gaston forced me to be here," he explained. "I'm too scared to go to Auradon."

The last student was Mad Maddy, one of Madam Mim's granddaughters. She had her namesake's wild hair and fierce expression. She too, looked balefully at the four Auradon representatives. "This is the roundtable thing, right? About getting into Auradon?"

"Yes, it is!" said Evie. "Please, take a seat." She glanced nervously over at Mal, and it seemed like Evie was wondering if Mal would be upset at seeing her old-friend-turned-enemy. But Mal just smirked and shrugged.

Mad Maddy took the other seat next to Ginny Gothel, and the two of them were soon whispering and cackling. Anthony looked bored and LeFou Deux kept fidgeting.

"I think this is it," said Jay, whispering to Mal. "We need to start, or we'll lose them too."

"Evie, did you want to start?" asked Mal.

"Sure!" said Evie, running up to the chalkboard to pull down a screen, which was also covered in dust. Once she stopped coughing, she turned to her friends. "Jay, the lights? Carlos, can you run the projector?"

"Since we can't bring you guys to Auradon Prep, we thought we'd bring Auradon Prep to you," said Evie, hitting PLAY on her computer to begin her slideshow. A photograph of the main castle building came on-screen, and the school song began playing in the background. The next slides showed earnest Auradon kids in classrooms, learning how to be good, the homecoming and tourney championship games, the marching band, and the cheer squad, along with various shots of ordinary life—students laughing, eating, and hanging out.

Jay turned the lights back on and was discomfited to find their entire audience had fallen asleep. He and Evie shared a distressed glance, and Carlos looked practically indignant.

"Is it over?" LeFou Deux blinked.

"Oh, thank Maleficent," said Ginny Gothel.

"What a snore," hissed Mad Maddy.

Anthony Tremaine was still asleep, his dark head resting on his arms on the table.

"Anthony, wake up, it's done," said Ginny Gothel, poking him awake.

Evie's smile faltered. "I just thought you might want to see what it's like," she said.

Jay patted her arm in consolation.

Mal crossed her arms and called the room to attention. "Thanks, Evie, that was really a wonderful peek into Auradon life, and I wish you guys had been paying attention." She narrowed her eyes at their audience. "*Anyway*, we wanted to talk to you guys about the VK program, and to see if you had any questions about Auradon."

Mad Maddy raised her hand immediately. "Oh! I have one! Can we use magic?"

"Yes!" said Mal, looking relieved that it was an easy question. "But it's discouraged and regulated."

Maddy's face fell. So did Ginny Gothel's. "What's the point, then?" asked Ginny.

"The point is to learn how to be a good person without having to resort to using magic. Magic makes people lazy and irresponsible," said Evie.

"Hmpf," said Ginny, who didn't look convinced. "Sounds dreary."

"So, what's Auradon Prep like?" asked Anthony Tremaine. "Why would we want to go there?"

"It's great! There are so many advanced classes, and it really prepares you for college," said Carlos.

"And so many extracurricular activities," said Evie. "What are you guys interested in?"

"Embezzling," said Anthony Tremaine.

"Poisons," said Ginny Gothel.

"Revenge," said Mad Maddy.

LeFou Deux just continued to look nervous. "Anything you guys think I would be interested in," he said, resorting to his usual flattery.

The rest of the discussion went the same way, frustrating both groups at the roundtable. At the end of the period, not one of the villains took an application form.

When they had the room back to themselves, Jay said what was on all their minds. "Well, that went well. *Not.*"

"Was the slideshow that boring?" asked Evie.

"It was the best! You even got Dude in there," said Carlos supportively.

"They don't understand. I thought they would if we came and spoke to them and they saw how we'd changed," said Mal. "Or maybe this is all a mistake. Maybe we're just wasting our time."

Evie turned to Mal and put both of her hands on Mal's shoulders. "Helping people and showing them another way to live—it's always worth our time. We can't give up yet. We'll figure out how to make them understand—how to make them *want* Auradon."

"Oh, they'll want it, I assure you," said Jay. "Evie's right, we'll figure it out. It's just that right now all they know is evil."

"So we have to sell them good," mused Carlos. "Show them how amazing it is."

chapter
22

Around the Island

After the meeting, the four of them split up—
Evie to see if she could find the remaining
members of the Anti-Heroes Club and convince them to
apply, Jay to follow up with Coach Gaston after practice,
Carlos to scout some locations for the Auradon Prep posters, and Mal to take a few pictures of the island to show
Ben how things were faring there. Except Mal didn't take a
camera with her. She didn't want to alarm her friends, but
she was truly worried about Celia's warning. She decided
to do a security sweep of the island to see if there was any
place in the invisible barrier that might have been weakened
by Uma.

As she walked around the island, Mal checked her pocket to make sure she still had the remote that opened the barrier and called up the bridge to the mainland. She felt a little spooked that this one small key could open up the island just like that, but that was the way its magic worked. Ben trusted her with it too. Still, though she had never worried about it before, she found that she kept making sure it was there.

So far, nothing seemed amiss on the island. There were no signs of any illicit magic around, and while she did find a trail of tentacle slime, it only led to Ursula's cottage, where Ursula was watching her "stories," aka the soap operas she watched on an old DVD player. The old sea witch was annoyed to see Mal at her doorstep.

"What do you want?" she rasped.

"Oh, hey, I was just wondering—Uma hasn't been around, has she? You haven't seen her?" asked Mal.

"No, last I saw her was on the news when she was blasting you with her magic!" Ursula laughed. "Good for her!"

"Um, yeah," said Mal. "Okay, just wanted to check."

"What do you want to see her for, anyway? Thought you guys weren't friends anymore," said Ursula suspiciously.

"Oh, nothing," said Mal. "Just curious is all."

She backed up, hoping Ursula wouldn't take a swipe at her with her tentacles. Ursula closed the door with a bang.

Mal was heading away when she realized she had no idea where she was going or where she had been. That was odd, wasn't it? It almost felt like she was daydreaming. She was standing on the sidewalk, a confused look on her face, when she bumped into Carlos.

"Hey, Mal!" said Carlos. "What's up? You all right?"

She shook off the weird feeling. Maybe she was just spooked to be back on the Isle of the Lost. Too many bad memories. "Yeah, I'm okay. What are you up to?"

"Oh, just figuring out the best places for the posters. I thought we should put up some Auradon Prep billboards too. Really inundate the place."

"Cool," said Mal.

"What about you? What are you doing so far from the hideout?" asked Carlos.

"Nothing," said Mal. She couldn't remember. What had she been doing? Maybe it wasn't important—that's why she couldn't remember.

"Well, I've got to check out a building over there. I think we can paste over your old 'Down with Auradon' signs," said Carlos apologetically. "See you later."

"Yeah, see you back at the hideout," said Mal. "Be careful."

"I will," promised Carlos.

Carlos watched Mal walk away. She seemed a bit off, but maybe she was just concentrating on something. She was Mal, and she could take care of herself. He didn't have to worry, did he?

Like Mal, Carlos hadn't been completely straight with the gang. Sure, he was scouting locations for posters and billboards, but he was also testing a system he had invented. Part of the graduation surprise he and Jane had cooked up. It had mostly been Jane's idea, but Carlos was the technical part of the operation.

He took out his phone and opened the new app he'd put on it. He studied the screen and grinned as it began to work.

Excitedly, he texted Jane.

C-Dog: *I think your surprise is going to work!*

Jaaaaane: *If you're texting me, it sure is! How's everything over there?*

C-Dog: *Okay. Glad we're going home soon. Isle kids don't really get the appeal of Auradon.*

Jaaaaane: *Maybe we need to make a bigger deal out of them.*

C-Dog: *?*

Jaaaaane: *Like a day to really celebrate the villain kids.*

C-Dog: *Oh like a VK Day!*

Jaaaaane: *Yes!*

C-Dog: *Evie will LOVE that idea. You're a genius!* ☺

Jaaaaane: *Okay I have to go. See you soon!*

C-Dog: *Counting down the minutes!*

She sent him a heart. Carlos looked at it for a long time, then put his phone away.

• • •

If Mal had noticed Carlos was being cagey earlier, she didn't give it much thought. She was too worried about the strange gap in her memory. She was walking through the bazaar, lost in her thoughts, when she bumped into Harriet Hook.

"Hey, Harriet," said Mal.

"Mal!" said Harriet. "Oh, I heard about your roundtable at study hall. My sister, CJ, kept bugging me to go, but I had a big test, and you know the Queen of Hearts threatens to chop off our heads if we fail."

"It's okay," said Mal. "You probably know all about Auradon from CJ."

Harriet gave Mal one of her rare smiles. "So, how did it go?"

Mal shrugged. "Not our finest hour," she admitted. "We couldn't get anyone to realize how great it is. Maybe they didn't want to hear it. Not everyone will get to go, after all."

"That's never stopped a determined bunch of villains before," said Harriet.

"You're right," said Mal. "Maybe we have the wrong approach. . . . Thanks!"

"No problem," said Harriet.

Mal began to walk away, but Harriet stopped her.

"Mal?" Harriet said. "You were headed that way," she said, pointing her fake hook in the opposite direction.

Mal startled. "I was?"

"Yeah. I'm the one going this way."

"Oh," said Mal. "Thanks!"

Mal twirled around, trying to hide her embarrassment. What was going on? Why was she acting like this? And why did she have a feeling it had something to do with Uma?

chapter
23

Pied Piper

That night, Mal lay in bed, thinking of Celia's warning and the strange gaps in her memory earlier that day. Was Uma out to get her? Of course she was. Uma was *always* out to get her. Uma had never forgiven Mal for, well, being Mal. Being the best at everything. At first, that meant being wicked. Then she hated Mal for being good and for being Ben's choice. But if Mal kept worrying about Uma, she would never go to bed. She tossed. She turned. She tossed again. Jay was sitting by the window, keeping watch. If anything happened, they would know. Mal relaxed, and slowly she went to sleep.

She dreamed she was back in her old home, sitting on

her bed. She was younger than she was now. She was a kid: maybe four, five years old. Her mother was in the kitchen, a cauldron was bubbling on the stove, and goblins were cowering at Maleficent's words because they had brought back the wrong ingredients for the soup. It could have been any other ordinary day.

Mal hadn't thought of her childhood in a long time. Why was she dreaming about it now?

Then the dream changed, and she was standing in front of the classroom at Dragon Hall. She was still a little kid, but now she was in third grade. She had just won the Wicked Prize. It was an award given to the most dastardly student of each grade level, and since kindergarten, Mal had always won. She was the baddest of the bad. Her mother had been so proud of her!

The little Mal in the dream went home to show her parents her prize.

That's our bad little girl.

Mal.

That voice.

That voice was so familiar. It was a voice she hadn't heard for a long time. *Mal . . .*

Mal sat up. Was she dreaming? Had she just heard a voice, or was she just imagining it? She fell back on the lumpy mattress. She wasn't hearing anything. It was completely silent in the hideout.

She closed her eyes and began to drift off once more.

Then she heard it again. *Mal . . . Hey, Mal . . . you know where to go. Come on.*

Mal's arms locked against her sides. Something was happening—something was compelling her to leave. But she wouldn't go.

Mal. Get up. That's an order.

Mal's eyes snapped open, a glazed look to them. She got up quietly. Her friends, including Jay, who was snoring by the windowsill, didn't stir. She had to go. *Now.*

chapter
24

A Dream Is a Wish Your Heart Makes?

Carlos shrank back from his mother in fear. Cruella
De Vil was annoyed, and when she was annoyed,
watch out. She paced the length of their ballroom, her
high heels clomping on the floor as her minions, Jasper and
Horace, cringed in front of her. Cruella hadn't seemed to
notice Carlos yet, but it was only a matter of time. "Where
are the puppies?!" she demanded. "Where are they?"

"They're gone! They've disappeared!" Jasper said, quak-
ing, while Horace hid behind him. Carlos curled tighter
into himself from where he was crouched against the wall.

Cruella paced the room, her fur coat trailing behind her

as she waved her long cigarette holder and dusted the furniture with ashes. "Those puppies are mine! Mine, I tell you! Find them!" she raged. "Bring me ALL THE PUPPIES! OR ELSE!"

Horace shook in his boots and wrung his hat. "We tried!"

"But they're nowhere!" said Jasper.

"They're gone!"

"Nooooo!" screamed Cruella. "CARLOS! CARLOS! CARLOS!"

Carlos woke up drenched in sweat, fully expecting to find himself back at Hell Hall, the family estate, his mother looming over him, her diamond bracelets rattling in his face, her lips set in a perpetual scowl as she puffed smoke rings in his direction.

But it was only Evie and Jay, looking concerned. "You had a nightmare," said Evie. "You were yelling."

"You woke us up," said Jay.

Outside the window of the loft, two people were arguing over a trinket they'd found on the street. "That's mine!"

"No, it's mine!"

"MINE!"

"Nooooo!"

The sounds of people squabbling always reminded Carlos of his mother, he realized. She would never stop haunting his dreams.

It was only when his heart had stopped pounding that he realized that there were just three of them in the hideout. "Where's Mal?" he asked.

Jay and Evie glanced around. "What?" said Jay.

"Omigosh!" Evie gasped. "I was asleep until I heard you, Carlos. Did either of you see her?"

They shook their heads. Evie dashed frantically around the room, overturning pillows and blankets. Mal's jacket and boots were missing too. Carlos scratched his head. "She's gone?"

Jay flushed. "I was supposed to be keeping watch!" he said. "But I was exhausted."

"It's not your fault," Evie said. "Don't blame yourself."

"But where would she have gone? And why didn't she tell us where she was going?" asked Carlos. An uneasy feeling crept over him.

"I don't know," said Evie. "It's not like her to do this. She knows we would worry."

Carlos looked around the dark loft. "Did she leave a note?"

"Let's check," said Evie, and the three of them searched the entirety of the loft. Jay even picked through the trash, which was still full of rotten pirate debris. But they didn't find anything. Not a word.

Carlos sighed. This was why he had been reluctant to go back to the island in the first place. He knew something like this would happen. It always did.

Then he heard Evie gasp. "Guys, check this out!" She pointed at the floor.

It was Mal's boot print, leading toward the door. But there was something strange about it. It seemed to have the slightest glow. Almost . . . blue.

"Uma," said Jay, his eyes narrowing. The others nodded in agreement. Whatever this was, it wasn't good. But at least it looked like there were tracks to follow.

Carlos pulled on his black-and-white leather jacket. "What are we waiting for?" he said. "Let's go. We've got to find her."

chapter

25

Once Upon a Dream

his way, Mal.
　　　Come on.
Hurry.

Mal followed the deep, strangely familiar voice that urged her out of the hideout into the deserted streets of the Isle of the Lost. She walked by the Slop Shop, down Mean Street, and past Gaston's cottage. She wandered in a daze, unsure if she was still dreaming and asleep on the mattress, or actually outside in the cold night air. She heard the crunch of gravel beneath her feet. Her head felt foggy. She was compelled to follow the voice, no matter what.

"Keep going," said a new voice, and when Mal looked up she saw Dizzy Tremaine, with her signature pigtails and oversize glasses, standing on the deserted sidewalk.

"Dizzy? What are you doing here?" asked Mal. What was she doing out here so late and so far from her home on Stepmother's Island? Dizzy shouldn't be out at this time of the night.

"Don't worry about me," Dizzy said with a laugh. "You just keep going, Mal. That way!" Dizzy threw her head back and cackled, and something glowed around her neck. She reminded Mal of someone. Who laughed like that? The answer was in the back of her mind, but she couldn't access it. It was like she was sleepwalking. Maybe she was.

"Where am I going?" she asked.

"You'll see," said Dizzy mysteriously. "You're almost there."

Mal bent down to tie her shoelace, and when she stood up Dizzy had disappeared. Had that even been Dizzy? What was going on? But she felt that she was going the right way. She had to continue.

She walked to the intersection of Pitty Lane and Bitter Boulevard, a route she had traveled countless times when she was a denizen of the Isle of the Lost. She remembered knocking down garden gnomes, pushing over mailboxes, tagging walls.

Then suddenly there was Gil, leaning against a wall, eating a rotten apple. "Oh, hey, Mal, keep going."

This was Mal's territory. What was a pirate doing here? It was like he appeared out of nowhere.

"Going where?"

Gil rolled his eyes. "Jailor's Pier. Where else?"

"What are you doing in my dream?" she asked.

"It's not a dream," said Gil. "It's real." Then he giggled maniacally. Mal thought he didn't sound like himself. . . . He sounded like . . .

But she couldn't finish the thought, so instead she kept walking toward the pier. When she was a little girl, she liked to play tricks on people there. She would throw a bucket of slime on the wood slats, making them slippery and sending unsuspecting villains sliding down the length of the pier and into the water. Mal hoped no one played a prank on her tonight. Seagulls lined the deck, picking at leftover trash. She walked to the end of the pier, where she came upon Harry Hook fishing, his line dangling out into the water. "Harry?" she asked hesitantly.

"Oi! Mal, there you are."

"Why am I here?" she asked, still not sure if this was really happening or even if that was truly Harry in front of her. Like Dizzy and Gil, there seemed to be something glowing around his neck.

"You should never have left," he said solemnly. "You should never have left the Isle of the Lost."

"What? And stay here with you?" Mal smirked.

"What's so terrible about that?" asked Harry, attempting to look wounded.

"Everything," Mal growled.

"Ouch." Harry disappeared in a blink. Mal stepped back. What just happened? Where did Harry go? And Gil? And Dizzy?

She ventured to the outskirts of town, right to the middle of a forest, in the deep dark heart of the woods, where a glowing blue orb floated in the middle of the darkness. And it spoke with a familiar voice.

Mal . . .

She turned away from the orb and kept walking through to the other side, and now she found herself at the opposite edge of the forest, close to the pier, and there was Dizzy again.

"Mal! What are you doing out here?" asked Dizzy.

Mal was confused. Didn't she just see Dizzy earlier? How did she get here so fast? She told Dizzy about walking out into the woods and seeing this blue orb.

"It spoke with a voice . . . and it sounded crazily like my . . ." *Dad?* Mal shook her head. "No, that's impossible," said Mal. "But what are *you* doing out here?"

"We were supposed to meet up at Curl Up and Dye hours ago, remember?" said Dizzy.

"We were?" Mal didn't remember making this plan.

"It's okay, I was just excited to . . ." Dizzy said, and

then she stopped and looked disoriented for a moment, as if unsure of where she was and what was happening.

"Dizzy? Are you okay?" asked Mal.

Dizzy jumped. "Of course I'm okay!" she said with a too-cheerful smile. "There's just so much glam to add in so little time!" She picked up Mal's hands. "Just because they're cuticles does not mean they're cute!" she said, and then stopped as if something was choking her.

Mal leaned over and gasped. "Dizzy! Why are you glowing?"

"Glowing?" asked Dizzy, and then she held her chest in pain.

There was something glowing around Dizzy's neck. Mal reached over and lifted the source of the light. It was a seashell necklace.

"Dizzy! Why are you wearing Uma's necklace?" she asked.

Dizzy looked down at the necklace, confused, but when she looked back up at Mal, there was a crafty smile on her face. It wasn't Dizzy's smile. Mal knew that smile.

"I wouldn't say that Dizzy's wearing my necklace," said a voice that was definitely not Dizzy's. "It's more like my necklace is wearing Dizzy!"

"Uma!" Mal said angrily. "This is so low! Your fight is with me, not Dizzy! And she's a child!"

"Oh, I can go lower, princess," said Uma as Dizzy. She took off Dizzy's glasses and stomped on them. "Oops!" She shrugged. "Just you wait."

Mal scoffed. Uma didn't scare her. "Am I supposed to be frightened?"

Just then Harry and Gil appeared out of nowhere and flanked Dizzy/Uma. Both of them had similar glowing lights at the bases of their throats.

Harry waved his hook in Mal's face. "You're not welcome on the Isle anymore!"

But Mal was simply amused. "Really? And what are you going to do about it, pal? Mr. . . . Coat Hanger?"

"His name is Harry," Gil said smugly. Then he realized. "Oh, I get it . . . because it looks like . . . That's pretty funny, Mal!"

Mal smirked. "Thanks. I'll be here all week."

"Uma's going to have the last laugh, though," said Gil, as the three of them began walking closer to Mal, and she had to walk backward, closer to the pier. "I wouldn't want to be you right now, Mal."

"I wouldn't want to be her ever," sneered Dizzy with Uma's voice.

The three of them kept inching forward as Mal kept walking backward, edging onto the pier, but now she was annoyed. "What makes you think this is going to be any different from every other time that I've beaten you?"

Now Harry spoke in Uma's voice. "Those were measly little battles. There's a war coming!"

"And in this war, I will triumph, I'll have everything—the Isle and Auradon!" said Gil in Uma's angry voice.

Uma was definitely getting worked up, wherever she was.

"And you, princess—I'm coming for you, Mal," said Uma menacingly through Dizzy.

Mal stood her ground, even as Harry unsheathed his sword and the three of them kept edging toward her in a threatening manner. "Mal . . . Mal . . . Mal . . ." they whispered, as they glowed with the light from Uma's seashell necklace.

"Oh yeah?" Mal said, curling her lip. She wasn't afraid of them, not now and not ever. "Not if I come for you first!"

With that, she turned away from them and began running down the pier. If Uma wanted a fight, Mal would bring it to her. She ran to the very end of the dock, determined to fight and vanquish Uma once and for all.

She leaped gracefully, throwing herself up in the air.

Then Mal heard a different voice shriek her name, but it was too late to turn around.

chapter
26

Underground Secrets

After trying to warn Mal and her friends, Celia decided to go back down the mine shaft to see what Uma and Hades were up to. Holding on to her hat, Celia ran to the basement tunnels until she reached the one that led to the mine shaft and Hades's cave.

She grabbed a torch and hopped onto an old rusty bicycle that was on the train tracks. She began pedaling furiously. Surely Mal would figure out some way to thwart Uma's plans after Celia had warned her about the danger. Celia hadn't realized just how much she wanted to go to Auradon Prep until the prospect had been put in jeopardy. She had to get off the Isle and make a name for herself somewhere it would matter. And she wanted to see the world beyond the barrier! There were so many places she had heard of but had never been. . . .

One day she would fly to Never Land and meet the pixies and the fairies of the hollow. Or she would tour the castles in the Auroria Priory and see how they compared to the ones in Cinderellasburg. But best of all she would travel to the bayou, to dance with an alligator who played trumpet in a jazz band. After hearing her dad's stories all those years, she was desperate to get a glimpse of it herself.

The VK program was her one shot to get everything she'd ever dreamed of. There was no future on the Isle of the Lost. Her cards always said so.

Her cards . . . She felt around for them in her pockets and realized she'd dropped them somewhere in the tunnel. She got off the bicycle and began to search, sweeping her flashlight to and fro, but they were nowhere to be found. She'd have to retrace her steps.

But just then the flashlight sputtered out—she had forgotten to replace the battery! Celia shook it in annoyance. To her surprise, she realized that without the beam, she could see light peeking in through tiny little cracks in the cave walls. She'd never noticed them before, but then, the flashlight had always worked before.

"Where are my cards?" she asked herself, and, almost like magic, her cards flew to her hand.

Almost like magic? she wondered. *Or magic itself?*

There was something going on down here. She could feel it in the darkness, in the pinpoints of light, in the way her cards hummed in her hands.

Hades. It had to be Hades. He still had some kind of power down here, magic that was getting in through the cracks. She could feel it vibrating in the air. Not enough magic to escape from the Isle of the Lost, but enough to do some kind of harm, she was sure. Even a little magic can cause a lot of problems. That's what her dad always said, with that evil grin of his.

Celia put a hand to the nearest crack in the wall. It was so deep that the light coming through was almost blinding. Little dust motes filled the air, and Celia felt her cards tremble in her hands. *Magic.* Celia could barely comprehend it, but it had to be true. How else had Uma been able to get in and out of Hades's lair without being seen?

If there was magic on the Isle of the Lost, what kind of mischief was afoot?

chapter
27

Search Party

They had been looking for Mal for what felt like hours, following her boot tracks, and now Evie was beginning to really worry. They had questioned every person they'd bumped into on the street—goons, thugs, witches, and goblins alike—but no one had seen Mal. They had walked the length of the island, from Hook's Bay to Troll Town to Doom Cove, using the Ricketty Bridge to get across the coastline. But there was no sign of her. And the last boot print they found had been several blocks away.

It was as if Mal had suddenly disappeared. "Guys, I think we need to call the palace and let Ben know that Mal's missing," said Evie. "We can't keep it from him. What if something terrible has happened to her?" If something terrible really had happened, Evie would never forgive herself.

"We can't. At least not yet. We'd have to go back to Auradon to tell him, which means leaving Mal here," said Jay. "Remember? There's no signal on the Isle. It's completely cut off."

Carlos was about to say something when Jay interrupted him. "Hey, look, the Slop Shop's open," he said, as they walked past the storefront. "Come on, let's ask if she stopped in here."

They walked into the goblin-run establishment. A few of Maleficent's minions had retired from their lives as henchmen to run a coffee shop. "Well, look who's back," said the head goblin barista as he polished some cups. "What are you guys doing here?"

"We're looking for Mal," said Carlos. "Have you seen her?"

"I thought you were here for that Auradon business," said the goblin cagily.

"Well, yes, but—" began Jay, but the goblin cut him off.

"Trying to get more kids to apply to Auradon Prep, huh?" he said. "What about goblins?" He wiped the counter with a dirty rag, making the surface even dirtier.

"Um . . ." said Carlos. "No, not yet, sorry." Jay picked up a plastic-wrapped scone that was hard as a rock. Evie gave him a look, and he set it back down.

"Our dwarf cousins said they'd put in a good word for us with the king. Guess they forgot about us," complained the goblin, shaking his green head.

"Okay, focus," said Evie with a strained smile. "Have you guys seen Mal? Did she go this way?"

"Yeah, she was here. Not in the shop, but I think a couple of demons mentioned that they saw her outside. Pain! Panic!" he called. "Come over here."

Two short demons ambled over. One was slurping a Sloppacino with a green straw. The other one was wearing what looked like slightly scorched plastic sandals with Hercules's face on them. "What's up?" Pain asked.

"Didn't you say you saw Mal?" asked the goblin.

"Yeah. She was talking to herself."

"What?" Carlos demanded.

"I know, I thought it was weird too! It was like she was talking to someone who wasn't there," said Panic. "Totally freaky."

"She looked like she was in a dream state, like sleep-walking," said Pain. "The way they do in the River Styx. Like they're dead—you know, when they float around all dead-eyed. That's what she looked like."

Evie looked alarmed. "Did you wake her?"

Pain and Panic shook their heads vigorously and hopped up and down. "Of course not! Are you kidding? Wake Mal? She'd curse us!" they protested. "Who would do such a stupid thing? Not us!"

"You guys, Mal really isn't like that anymore. Trust me," said Evie. "She wouldn't harm a fly . . . or a demon."

"Well, we weren't going to take any chances," said Pain stubbornly. Panic nodded vigorously.

"Which way was she going?" asked Carlos.

Panic pointed east. "Kind of down thataway, toward the harbor."

They walked toward the direction the demons pointed, down Mean Street, past the bazaar and Frollo's house, but the streets were empty. Jay was starting to think that the demons had deliberately sent them the wrong way.

"Mal doesn't sleepwalk," said Evie. "She's been my roommate for years. I've never seen her do that."

"They said she looked dead-eyed. You think maybe she was under some kind of spell?" mused Carlos.

"But if there's no magic on the Isle of the Lost, how could that be?" asked Evie.

"Maybe someone figured out how to get past the barrier," said Carlos, as Jay suddenly stopped and knelt to examine something on the path.

"Look," he said, pointing past an upturned barrel to a mark on the dirt road. It was a perfect print of a boot with a serpent coiled around the heel mark. The same prints they had been following all evening. There was another one not too far away, and then the tracks picked up again. The three of them hurried to follow.

They followed the tracks all the way to Jailor's Pier. "The demons weren't lying after all. She was headed to the harbor," said Jay. He glanced toward the end of the dock and then broke out into a flat-out run.

"What's going on?" asked Evie.

"There's MAL!" said Carlos, pointing to the edge of the dock.

chapter

28

All Washed-up

Jay froze in place for a moment, then bolted toward Mal, with Evie and Carlos close behind him. Mal was facing toward them, but it seemed like she was arguing with someone. Jay thought he heard her say, "Not if I come for you first." But what did that mean? Who was she speaking to?

"MAL! What are you doing?" screamed Evie.

"MAL!" Jay yelled. He had to wake her up. She was definitely sleeping or dreaming, or something weird was going on. That wasn't the Mal they knew. He was blaming himself for anything that might have happened; he was supposed to be here to protect his friends. Sure, they could all take care of themselves, but he was the one with the swords-and-shields expertise; he was supposed to try to keep everyone safe. Even Mal, who had never needed any help. But she sure did now.

Because it was like Mal didn't—couldn't—hear them. She turned on her heel and sprinted toward the end of the pier.

"MAL!" The three of them were screaming now. "MAL, STOP!"

But it was too late. Mal threw herself off the pier and plummeted all the way down into the sea.

Jay dived into the water right after her, spinning around in a complete circle, searching for any sign of his friend. The sea was a brilliant shade of blue, which was rare for Isle water. He had expected it to be almost completely murky, but it was crystal clear. He should have been able to spy her the moment he jumped in.

But Mal was nowhere to be found. It was as if she had jumped into the ocean and out of this world. Suddenly, a great swarm of fish surrounded him, dark as the night, obscuring his vision.

He could hardly see the hand he held out in front of his face. There were thousands of the little fish, each one twisting and turning, going this way and that, making it impossible to see anything at all. Jay got the feeling someone was trying to stop him from finding Mal. Most likely the same person who had compelled her to jump off the pier.

Jay held his breath and swam as deep as he could go, but the fish followed, surrounding him like fog, hindering his ability to see. *Useless*, he thought. Someone was determined to keep him from finding Mal. Jay swam back to shore, gasping for air when he broke the surface.

Evie and Carlos looked down at Jay from the edge of the pier, panic on their faces. "Where is she?" asked Evie.

"Couldn't find her. Just needed to take a breath," he said. "I'll go back down and search again."

"Hold on," said Evie. "I've been thinking of what Carlos said. About how Mal might be under a spell."

"Yeah, it's like she was enchanted," said Carlos.

"A spell?" asked Jay. "Here? On the Isle? Impossible."

"I know, but when has the impossible ever been an obstacle for magic?" said Evie. "Someone must have found a way around the barrier and is using their magic against Mal."

"If there's magic here, it's definitely working against us too," said Jay. "A school of fish was blocking my vision down there. That's probably not a coincidence."

"Yeah, I don't think you'll be able to find her if you dive back down," said Evie.

"So what are we going to do about it?" asked Jay, climbing the makeshift rope ladder at the end of the pier.

"Already on it," said Evie, as Carlos reached out a hand and helped pull Jay back onto the pier. He shook the water from his long hair and wrung it from his jacket.

"What's the plan?" Jay asked.

"We're going home," said Evie. "To my castle. If there's magic on the Isle, I think I know how to fight it."

"Um, your castle is also the home of Evil Queen. I've heard she doesn't like guests," said Carlos.

"Where did you hear that?" teased Jay.

"From Evie," said Carlos.

Evie brushed their jokes aside as they walked down the pier. "Oh, don't worry about Mom. It's game night, when she plays Apples to Apples with her friends. Actually, I think they call it Rotten Apples to Rotten Apples. Or maybe it's Poisoned Apples to Poisoned Apples? I can't remember."

"Charming," said Carlos. "So the castle's empty?" he asked, looking greatly relieved.

"Like a schoolroom after last bell," said Evie. "We'll be all alone, but we better hurry. Mom doesn't stay out late. She likes her beauty sleep."

chapter
29

Under the Sea

Mal heard her friends calling her name, but it was too late. She had already jumped. She fell straight down into the sea, so deep that a wave of bubbles washed up all around her. She opened her eyes and gasped, fearing she would drown, but no water entered her throat. The person who had led her down there wanted her alive.

Uma.

Mal should have known to take Celia's warning more seriously. She should have known that Uma would go to any length to get revenge. Mal didn't know how she had done it, but Uma had managed to get back to the Isle of the Lost, and she'd somehow accessed enough magic to lure Mal away from her friends and trap her under the sea. Mal couldn't believe Uma would stoop so low as to use Dizzy, Gil, and Harry to fool her, though. Actually, it was Uma. Uma might not have gotten the crown she'd always wanted, but she was the queen of reaching new lows.

Mal tried to swim to the surface, but she discovered she had landed in the middle of a school of fish. They swam around her like a floating wall, keeping her from getting her bearings. When they disappeared she was alone, under-water, and in the dark.

She kept falling deeper and deeper, until she was at the bottom of the sea, standing on what appeared to be the wreck of some old pirate ship.

Mal whirled around, and, sure enough, her old nemesis was standing in front of her.

Uma threw her head back and cackled wildly. "There you are! Exactly where I want you!"

She was standing across from Mal, but she wasn't really there. It was as if Mal were looking into a mirror, except instead of seeing herself, she saw Uma reflected back at her.

Mal pursed her lips and crossed her arms. She wasn't about to play these games. "Uma, next time you want to talk to me, maybe you can just send a text? You do know they have those waterproof phones now, so even fish folk like you can have civilized conversations with the rest of us."

"This isn't a joke," said Uma.

Mal smirked at her old-friend-turned-enemy. "Oh, Uma, maybe you've just lost your sense of humor. Defeat has that effect on people." Mal's eyes glittered dragon green. She could sense the magic all around, but how was it possible so close to the Isle of the Lost? What had Uma done? And what did she want?

"She who laughs last, laughs longest," vowed Uma, as the pirate ship buckled underneath Mal's feet.

Uma's laughing face appeared in every bubble that rushed up around her, mocking Mal.

The deck cracked in two, a few boards tearing loose, and Mal flew back before they smacked into her. "Nice try," she said. "But you didn't really think it would be that easy, did you?"

Uma seethed. "Let's try this again, then, shall we?" she said through gritted teeth. With a whirlwind of force, she transformed into her octopus self. Her tentacle arms reached out for Mal, wrapping around her as if they were searching for something. One tentacle darted toward Mal's pocket.

What's she looking for? What does she want? Mal wondered. Then she realized: *She's looking for the key.* The remote that would open the barrier and call up the bridge to Auradon. Jay usually carried it as he sometimes drove the limo, but he didn't this time, because Mal wanted to keep it close to her for safekeeping. It was part of the new security protocols.

So that's what Uma was after. Uma has always wanted

the same thing—freedom from their island prison. Freedom to do as she pleased, to rampage and rage and spread her evil and her malice across the innocent kingdoms of Auradon.

Well, Uma would have to think again. It wasn't happening—not now, not ever. Especially not if Mal had anything to do with it.

"Really, Uma?" she said. "You're never going to beat me. What makes you think you're going to win this time?"

"I wouldn't be so cocky, Mal," Uma replied. "And let's evaluate for just a second. Who's the one with the upper hand here?" She grinned and waved a tentacle in Mal's face.

With a sudden burst of energy, Mal twisted away from Uma's grasp. She felt her eyes flash bright green again, and then she transformed into a great and towering dragon. Her arms became wings, and her fingers sprouted mighty talons. Her teeth turned to fangs, scales replaced her skin, and her long purple hair became a row of fierce spikes down her back.

Uma sneered and drew herself up again, her tentacles reaching out for Mal, but Mal flew back, using her wings to push herself through the water and narrowly avoiding being caught in Uma's grasp.

Uma spun, transformed back into her human form, and lurched away from Mal. Mal swam, chasing Uma, but Uma kept disappearing, changing from a squid to an octopus to a girl, darting into coral reefs and then transforming back into a humongous sea creature. *She's trying to lead me somewhere,* thought Mal. *But where? And why?*

Then Uma was back on the deck of the pirate ship, appearing suddenly in her human form and wielding a sword. Mal transformed back as well and landed on the ship. There on the ground was a discarded sword, and Mal lunged for it and grasped it in her hands. She faced Uma, her blade raised.

"So, we're doing this?" asked Mal.

"Oh, it's on," vowed Uma.

They battled up and down the deck, steel against steel.

"Just give me the key," said Uma. "And I'll let you go."

"You're not holding me anywhere," said Mal.

"One word and you'll drown," threatened Uma.

"Say it then!" said Mal. "Do it!"

Uma backed away as Mal relentlessly pushed forward, slashing and fighting so strongly that she forced Uma to drop her weapon.

Mal brought her sword under Uma's chin. "Are we done now?" she growled. But Uma suddenly disappeared, and her image appeared in a golden mirror that materialized on the deck.

Uma laughed at Mal's confusion.

Then Mal was back on the deck of the sunken pirate ship, standing in front of a door with a brass handle.

"UMA! FACE ME!" Mal demanded, reaching for the handle as the ocean reverberated with Uma's laughter.

chapter
30

With a Little Help from Her Friends

It was impossible to imagine that Evil Queen's castle could appear scarier and more foreboding than it already was, but somehow, it had managed to pull off this feat. It loomed above the crag, its dark tower rising to the skies. Evie remembered her lonely childhood spent inside its confines, her only company a mother obsessed with outward appearances. Evie knew every cosmetic trick, every fashion tip, but had been bereft of true support and affection. But this was no time for bad memories or a pity party. Mal was lost under the ocean, trapped by some evil force, and they had to help her.

The VKs made their way toward the castle, fighting

through a row of hedges and vines that surrounded its walls. "Ouch," said Jay, as he pulled a particularly large barb from his leg.

"Sorry," said Evie. "Mom prefers thorns and cuts off the roses."

"Of course," said Carlos. "Why are we here again?"

"If there's wicked magic on the Isle, then we need to fight it with similarly strong magic. And there's no magic stronger than in my mom's Magic Mirror."

"Isn't it broken?" asked Carlos.

"The glass is broken, and I have a tiny shard of it in my compact. But the frame still stands, and something tells me the glass was mostly for display. It's made of magic. And if there's magic on the Isle, it'll work."

They reached the drawbridge, passed over the moat, and stood in front of the main door. Evie felt in her pockets for the key and realized she'd left it back in her room on Auradon. She hadn't planned on visiting home.

"Guys, I have bad news," she told them. "I didn't bring the key."

"What now?" asked Carlos.

"Break in? Can't be that hard," said Jay with a shrug.

Evie shook her head. "Mom has massive security on this thing. Remember? This isn't Auradon. If we pick the lock and open the door without the right key, a steel trap will spring, and we'll all fall into a basement full of hungry alligators." It was the Evil Queen's castle, after all.

"Okay, so let's not do that," Carlos said with a shudder.

"Mom keeps a spare key in the vultures' nest, over there," Evie said, motioning to a ledge high in the air where they could just make out a shadow of a large bird's nest.

"Easy enough to climb," said Jay, starting to find a foothold in the castle walls.

"No!" screamed Evie, and Jay slid back to the ground.

"Sorry," she said. "The vultures will peck you to death. We'll just have to convince them I'm my mom."

Jay picked himself up and dusted off. "How're we going to do that?"

Evie smiled. "Makeup."

Evie knelt at the doorway, set down her purse, and began to remove assorted cosmetics from its depths—a dizzying array of lipstick, foundation, blush, eyeliner, and every conceivable beauty instrument known to humanity. She turned her back to the boys and began the transformation.

The eyebrows were easy, since she and her mother had the same dark brows. Evie just had to color them in so they looked more menacing. Then she covered her face in a pale powder and darkened her lips to bloodred. As a final touch, she fashioned a black scarf she found in her bag into a black cape.

When she turned to Jay and Carlos, the two of them staggered back.

"Whoa!" said Carlos. "You are way too good at that."

"Who are you, and what did you do with Evie?" said Jay.

Evie cackled like her mother and held out an apple she'd packed as a snack. "One bite and all your dreams will come true!" she purred in her best Evil Queen voice.

"Seriously, stop it!" yelled Carlos.

Evie giggled and sounded like her normal self. "Okay, fine." She fluffed up her cape and checked her appearance in her phone's camera. "I look like Mom, right? Enough to fool those old vultures?"

"Totally," said Jay.

"Could've fooled us," said Carlos.

She began to climb up the castle walls toward the vultures' nest, lifting herself up inch by inch. When she reached the ledge she smiled sweetly at the hungry birds of prey. Her mother's favorite pets.

"Hello, my dearies," she said in her best mimicry of her mother's voice. "I seem to have forgotten my keys! Now let me just . . ." She reached into the nest. The closest vulture lunged, snapping at her fingers.

Evie frowned. It looked like she would have to channel more of her mother after all. She couldn't just put on the makeup and expect the vultures to let her have the key. She had to *be* Evil Queen. The vultures began to shriek and caw at her.

"SILENCE!" she demanded. "You know the penalty if you fail to give me the key!" She glared at them as her mother would.

She looked so frightening and so much like her mother at that moment that the vultures squawked and flapped their wings, flying away from her as fast as they could.

"Sorry, birdies," Evie whispered as she reached back into the nest and grabbed the key to the front door.

She slid down, Jay and Carlos giving her a hand as she made it back to the front steps. In a blink, they were finally inside.

It was the same as it ever was, dark and shadowy and full of cobwebs. They tiptoed past the kitchen. "This place gives me the creeps," said Carlos. Jay nodded silently.

"Oh, it's not that bad," said Evie. "It's worse when Mom's around."

They made their way through the dark corridors up to the bedrooms, where Evil Queen kept her legendary Magic Mirror. Evie opened the door, half expecting her mother to scold her for letting in a draft. But it was as empty as expected. Mom never missed a night out with her hags.

The mirror's shards clung to the edges of the frame, but when Evie stepped up to it, it was almost as if it were whole again.

"Magic," whispered Evie. "I can feel it coming from below, from deep underground, somehow. It's weak, but it's working."

She gazed into the largest fragment. She noticed she was still wearing her Evil Queen disguise, which might turn out in their favor.

"Magic Mirror, from the farthest space, through wind and darkness, I summon thee!" she called.

For a moment the mirror remained foggy and dark, but slowly it began to shift and reveal something else: a face in the mirror. The face *of* the mirror.

"What wouldst you know, my queen?" asked the mirror in a deep, sonorous voice that echoed throughout the castle.

It worked! Evie tried to keep her composure.

"Magic Mirror on the wall," she said, addressing the mirror by its full, true name. "Show me the dark fairy named Mal."

The clouds swirled once more. Then they parted to reveal deep blue depths. A sunken pirate ship. A great school of fish, swimming in a circle.

"Where is she?" said Evie, searching every image in the mirror. "SHOW ME MAL!" she commanded.

Carlos gasped. "Look!"

Through the bubbles and the murk, they saw their friend walking dazedly on the deck of the ship. Mal was walking toward a door, as if compelled toward it.

She had a glassy look in her eyes as she reached for the handle.

"Mal! Stop! Don't open that door!" yelled Evie.

chapter
31

Open and Out

*B*ack in Hades's cave, Uma had suddenly returned, and was dripping water all over the floor. She was back from her battle with Mal—but the most important part was still to come.

"Hey! Watch it!" said Hades grumpily.

"I got her where I want her!" said Uma. "See!" She touched her seashell necklace and pointed toward the broken television, which sprang to life. It showed Mal under the sea, on the deck of a pirate ship, heading to a locked door.

"She thinks she won, but when she opens that door," said Uma gleefully, "I'll appear right in front of her, and then I'll take the key to our freedom! She's walking right into my trap!"

"She is?" asked Hades.

"Of course she is! I confused her, then spelled her, and now she's on the verge of letting all of us out!" Uma laughed in glee.

"How'd you do that?"

"I'm a sea witch," said Uma smugly. "I own these waves."

"Right!" said Hades, who appeared to finally catch on that their plan was working.

Uma plopped down on the couch and leaned back. "All she has to do is open that door."

Hades squinted at the screen. "What door?"

"That door!" said Uma, pointing to the door on the pirate ship, annoyed that she had to explain it again. "She opens that door and I pop out!"

"Really?" Hades asked, not quite convinced. "But you're here."

"When she opens the door, I'll be there! Sheesh, you're so slow. I think you spent too much time in the Underworld," said Uma.

"So you pop over there, and then what happens?"

"I grab the key to our freedom!" screeched Uma. "Click—open and out!" She glanced sideways at him. "What's wrong? You don't seem excited to leave."

"Oh, I am! I really am!" he said. But there was something else in his voice that Uma couldn't quite place.

Then Hades's face broke into a malicious grin. "Wait till I surprise my brother Zeus. He won't see me coming!"

"And I'll have my pirates back!" said Uma. She jumped off the couch and knelt by the television screen, her face inches from Mal's pixelated one.

"Come on, Mal!" she said.

"Mal, do it!" said Hades, joining her.

"MAL! OPEN IT! OPEN THAT DOOR!" they chorused.

chapter
32

Friendly Force

Through the mirror, Mal's friends watched in horror as she reached for the door handle.

"NO!!!" Carlos screamed, just as loudly as Evie. "MAL! DON'T OPEN IT!!!" He was sure they didn't want to know what was behind that door. And he was even more certain that Uma was behind this . . . whatever this was. Maybe Uma was even *literally* behind it. He wouldn't put it past her.

"We need to stop her!" yelled Jay.

"The mirror!" said Evie. She ran up to its frame and thrust an arm into it, bracing herself for a shattering of glass. Carlos sucked in his breath, and Jay lunged for Evie to pull her back. But her arm disappeared beyond the glass. Carlos could feel the water as it splashed out from the frame, cool and wet against his skin.

"Hold on, Mal! We're coming to get you!" Carlos said, as Evie climbed into the mirror and half of her body disappeared through it.

"Evie! Be careful!" said Jay, right behind her.

"Mal!" Evie cried as Mal reached out toward the handle of the door. "Don't open it!"

But Mal didn't hear. She just kept walking closer and closer to the door, and finally she pushed it open.

Now Uma stood in the doorway, cackling. She had a gleeful look on her face. "Give it to me!" she ordered, reaching for Mal's pockets.

Uma was fast, but Evie was even faster. She shoved her entire body through the mirror, through time and space. She became a force in the water that pushed Mal away from Uma as hard as she could.

All of a sudden, Mal shot back up to the surface, away from Uma, out of danger.

Uma screamed in anger and turned around, just as Evie's entire body fell through the mirror and appeared underwater, on the deck of the ship. Uma's face darkened. She extended a tentacle, grabbed Evie's wrist, and began to pull her into the abyss.

"Help!" cried Evie.

Carlos lunged into the mirror, grabbed Evie's legs, and

started pulling her back, so that she was halfway in and halfway out of the mirror. Jay grabbed Carlos and pulled both of his friends backward, trying to drag them back into the castle and out of the water.

Uma was strong, but they were stronger.

Together the three of them pulled with all their might.

They pulled so hard that they went tumbling backward, out of the mirror, landing with a splash on the floor of Evil Queen's castle.

"Mal!" yelled Evie, jumping to her feet. "She got away!"

"We did it!" Carlos shouted. Jay whooped.

Evie cheered and then glanced around the room. They were covered in seaweed. "Are you guys all right?"

Carlos nodded, trying to catch his breath. "I think so."

"Yeah, I'm good," said Jay, getting up from the puddle.

"Um, guys, what just happened?" said Carlos.

"The door . . ." started Evie, but then her eyes began to glaze over. Suddenly Carlos felt his memory slipping away. He blinked, confused, and touched his soaking-wet hair. What had Evie been about to say to them? And why were they all dripping with water?

"Yeah, what are we doing here?" asked Jay. "Where are we?"

Carlos and Evie stared back at him with matching blank expressions. "I have absolutely no idea," said Carlos. He felt like he had just woken up from an extremely vivid dream.

"Something with . . . the Magic Mirror, maybe?" Evie guessed, since they were standing right in front of it.

Carlos stared at the Magic Mirror. It was dark and broken. And it felt like he had been looking into it. Had he imagined that he had seen something there? But that couldn't be right—the mirror needed magic to work.

"We're in my home. But why?" Evie continued.

"We were looking for Mal? I think?" Carlos said, his forehead scrunching.

"Did we find her?" asked Evie.

"I hope so," said Jay.

"We've got bigger problems, boys," said Evie, as they heard the front door creak open. "We need to get out of here. My mom's home!"

chapter
33

Fortune-Teller

*T*he more Celia stared at the cracks in the cave wall, the more she was certain they weren't just fissures in the stone. There was a rip in the fabric of their world—this was a broken seam, spilling magic into the tunnels underneath the Isle of the Lost. Uma and Hades must have been counting on this tiny bit of magic to take Mal and her friends by surprise. *If only Dizzy were here,* Celia thought despairingly. She could help her figure out what to do.

Celia traced the spiderweb of cracks along the cave wall. There were so many of them, and it looked like they were spreading. What could she do? How could she fix a spell? She was nothing but a two-bit hustler, making up fortunes for people silly enough to pay for them. She couldn't help Mal and her friends.

She shuffled and reshuffled her cards out of habit. Then she realized—if there really was magic down here, she could use it. She sat down on the cold cave floor, cutting and shuffling her cards. She would read her own fortune, to guide her hand and find a solution. For once, her tricks might actually work.

How do I fix the cracks? she asked the cards as she shuffled them again and again, her hands shaking from nerves.

Celia placed three cards in front of her.

The first card was the Magician. Her past.

The next was the Queen of Wands. Her present.

The third was the Hermit. Her future.

What did it mean? The Magician was her past. A strong presence—her father, she thought. The great manipulator, a true magician. The second card represented who she was: the Queen of Wands, a sorceress in her own right. Someone dependable. A person others could count on. The third was the Hermit—an inward-looking card, one that represented a person's inner life.

Then she realized: It meant the ability to fix this rested within her. She didn't need anyone's help. She had the power all along.

Celia was her father's daughter. Dr. Facilier wasn't just the headmaster of Dragon Hall—he was a powerful witch doctor who had friends on the other side, including one particular friend who was very close indeed. She knew what she had to do.

A spell to fix a spell.

She called on her shadow, the creature that lived in her. Her shadow peeled herself away from Celia and turned to her. "What is your command, mistress?"

"Seal the spaces in between; weave the fabric of the barrier's spell back to its rightful strength; and where there is light, let darkness rule," Celia ordered. "Cast yourself wide and dark and deep."

Her shadow nodded, and then leaped onto the wall. It grew until it covered the cave in darkness, and one by one, every thread of light in the cave blinked out.

Celia held her cards. They did not tremble, nor did they call. The magic was snuffed out like a candle, by a shadow.

Celia felt herself gasp with relief, and she hugged her cards to her chest. Then, just as quickly, she brushed herself off and stood, pulling herself back together. *After that, I better get picked to go to Auradon Prep,* Celia said to herself as she worked her way back through the tunnel. *Imagine what I could do with real magic at my fingertips!*

chapter
34

Mermaids and Makeovers

*L*ike a curtain closing on a stage, everything suddenly disappeared—the bubbles, the pirate ship, the door—at the same time that an invisible force pushed Mal away and sent her flying off to safety.

"Face it, Uma, I'll always be stronger than you!" said Mal as the waves carried her away.

She could hear Uma's cry of rage from deep below echoing in the waves. "You, strong enough? In your dreams!!!" screamed Uma.

Mal shut her eyes.

When she opened them, she was standing at the pier again, and it was as if she had never fallen into the water.

Her memory was fading as well. She fought to hold on to fragments of images—the school of fish that had surrounded her, Uma's face laughing in all the bubbles, the pirate ship, a mirror, and that strangely compelling door.

Uma! Uma had been standing at the doorway, and she wanted something. Something Mal had.

Mal checked her pocket for the remote. It was still there. She sighed in relief.

Who had pushed Mal away from the door and brought her back to safety? It could only be some kind of friend or ally. She dimly recalled hearing Evie's voice calling to her, along with Jay and Carlos yelling.

Her friends had helped her. They had her back somehow. They had carried Mal away from Uma. She didn't know how they'd managed it, but deep in her heart, she knew they were the ones who'd gotten her to safety. If only she could remember what had really happened down under the waves. Yet, as she stood on the dock, she had already begun to forget what she was trying to recall.

She was standing on the dock when Dizzy appeared in front of her once more.

"Dizzy?" she asked uncertainly.

"Yeah, who else would it be? Are you okay?" asked Dizzy.

"It's the strangest thing. I was walking through the woods, and I came across this glowing orb thing and . . ." Had she told Dizzy this already? Why did she feel such déjà vu? "And you were Uma—you were speaking in Uma's voice. Then I was underwater, but I could swim."

Dizzy frowned. "Ohhhhkay, maybe you shouldn't go back to Auradon just yet. I could give you a makeover! That'll make you feel better."

Mal was still confused. Then she saw something in Dizzy's hand. She reached for it and studied it.

"You like?" asked Dizzy, offering it to Mal.

It was a seashell necklace.

"Actually, no, I think it might clash with your outfit," said Dizzy, taking it back.

Then that familiar voice whispered from the woods. *Mal* . . .

This time, Dizzy heard it too. "Did you hear that?" she asked nervously.

Mal looked all around, chills running up and down her spine. She knew that voice. "Dizzy, I think we might want to get out of here," she said. "There's danger coming. I can feel it. And I think it might be headed for Auradon." She took Dizzy's hand and led her away from the shoreline.

Then Mal took the seashell necklace from Dizzy, threw it on the ground, and stepped on it.

chapter
35

What Villains Want

When Evie, Jay, and Carlos arrived back at the hideout, Mal was already there, safe and sound. Evie felt a huge rush of relief at the sight of her friend. She hadn't realized she was so worried until the weight of it fell away. She ran up to Mal and gave her a quick hug.

"Where were you guys?" Mal asked, returning Evie's hug with a grateful expression.

"Looking for you!" said Jay, giving her a fist-bump. "We went around the whole island!"

"Your hair!" said Evie, pulling away to look at it from an objective distance. "You got a haircut?"

Mal patted her new wavy locks, now cut into a long bob. "I ran into Dizzy."

"That girl is a genius," said Evie admiringly.

"You like?" asked Mal.

"Love," affirmed Evie.

"A haircut? At this time of night?" asked Carlos. "I'll never understand women."

The girls laughed. Then Mal turned to Evie and stared at her closely. "Um, Evie? You know you really look like your mom?" asked Mal.

Evie ran to the nearest mirror. "I do! Isn't that weird? I never wear my makeup this way. I should get it off before I frighten any children."

"Well, we're glad you're safe. That we're all safe," said Jay.

"Safe on the Isle of the Lost. Now that's new," said Carlos with a grin. "Oh, by the way, I have an idea on how to get more kids to apply to Auradon Prep."

"You do? What is it?" asked Evie.

"I think we're going about this all wrong. What do villains like?" asked Carlos.

"Fame," said Mal.

"Riches," said Jay.

"Attention," said Evie.

"Exactly! So we have to sell it to them as a way to get all those. Not learning how to be good or being part of a team—they're not interested in that. Not yet. But they'll understand the appeal of a celebration."

"VK Day!" said Evie.

"Funny, that's what I called it too!" said Carlos. "But Jane's the one who came up with the idea."

"I knew there was a reason why I always liked her," said Evie. "Anyway, we'll tell Dr. Facilier that there'll be a huge party, and that the four kids who are chosen will be famous!"

The four of them turned to each other with just-slightly-wicked smiles on their faces. They knew this would work.

The next morning, they met with Dr. Facilier at Dragon Hall once more.

"Before we leave, we just wanted to share with you a new development concerning the VK program," said Mal.

"Oh? A new development, is there? Pray tell," said the witch doctor with his frightening smile.

"Tell him, Evie," said Mal.

Evie leaned forward, her voice a little breathless. "The four chosen kids will be celebrated with a huge, kingdom-wide feast that will be bigger and more spectacular than anything anyone has ever seen."

"We'll have a marching band, the royal family. . . . It will be an amazing welcome," said Mal.

"Talk about rolling out the red carpet," said Jay.

"The gold carpet," Carlos said with a wink.

Dr. Facilier nodded, and his eyes shone with greed. "I will make sure to tell the students of this new, very exciting development."

"See that you do. We'll be back in a few months to collect applications and announce the selected kids," said Mal.

chapter
36

Trickster Sister

A royal limousine flying blue-and-gold Auradon flags was waiting for them when they walked out of Dragon Hall, and a group of students were milling about, gawking at it. Mal felt a bit self-conscious at the sight of the luxurious vehicle, but tried not to show it. They had already picked up their trunks from the hideout, so they were ready to go. All they had to do was open the barrier and call up the bridge, and they would be back in Auradon in no time.

"Home, Jay," Mal said to her friend with a wink as she climbed into the limo. Jay slid into the driver's seat, grinning.

"Finally," said Evie, climbing in next to her.

"Ditto," said Carlos.

"Let's blow this joint," said Jay, honking the horn. "Isle of the *Get Lost*."

Mal nodded. "I'm glad we're on our way. I have this weird feeling that we need to be back in Auradon as soon as we can. I might even have Ben cancel the rest of my official visits. I want to be on guard," she said, a determined look on her face.

"It'll be fine. You're just spooked because we're back here," Carlos said. "Evil lurks in every corner on the Isle. Really, I think I just saw Claudine Frollo over there."

"Nah, Mal's right. It's good we're heading back now. Besides, we have to get ready for graduation," said Jay.

"Graduation!" cried Evie. "Finals are coming up! And I still have to make all the caps and gowns!"

Jay was about to roll up the window when they saw Celia emerge from a manhole cover, top hat first.

"Oh, hi," she said, nonchalantly, as if she often emerged from subterranean levels.

"Hey, what's up?" said Mal. She stared at Celia. There was something odd about her, but she couldn't quite place it.

"Everything okay?" called Evie.

"I think so," said Celia. "You guys are fine, right?"

"We are," said Mal. She still wasn't sure what had happened the night before, but she knew she had faced and survived some sort of danger.

"Good." Celia leaned over to talk to Evie through the window. "That last card I told you about?" she said. "When I read your fortune?"

"Yes?" asked Evie warily.

"It doesn't just mean disaster. I mean, it doesn't mean disaster at all. It just means change," said Celia. "Sorry I made it sound like a bad fortune."

Evie brightened. "Change, huh? So change is in my future?"

"Pretty much," said Celia.

"Well, I am graduating in a few weeks," said Evie. "So there's going to be a lot of change happening."

Celia yelped. "I was right? I predicted it correctly? That's so cool!"

Evie laughed. "You did. Thanks, Celia."

Celia rewarded Evie with a huge smile. Then she turned to face all of them. "Headed back to Auradon now?" she asked wistfully.

Mal nodded. "Yeah."

"But we'll be back," said Evie.

"Soon," added Carlos.

"We promise," said Jay.

"I hope so," said Celia, tipping her hat to them.

They waved to Celia until she was just a dot on the horizon and the car was speeding on the bridge back to the mainland. Carlos raided the treats in the limousine, happy to find it was still stocked with as much chocolate and candy as always. Mal looked out the window as the island grew smaller and smaller in the distance.

"I'll call it. This was a success," said Carlos. "We got the applications out. Now we just wait to see them come in."

Jay smiled at them in the rearview mirror. "They will. Dr. Facilier was practically drooling at the thought of VK Day."

"To villains!" said Carlos with a cackle. He put out his hand. "Come on, make the pile," he said to Mal and Evie.

One by one they put their hands on top of one another's. Jay met their eyes in the mirror and nodded.

"The Isle of the Lost will always be home," said Evie. "It's where we're from."

"But we're also from Auradon now," said Mal. She had grown up a child of the Isle of the Lost, a mean-spirited, selfish little sprite, but now she was a defender of Auradon, a lady and a dragon. She wasn't only Maleficent's daughter or King Ben's girlfriend. She was also just Mal.

"I'll always be just Mal," Mal murmured.

"'Just Mal'?" asked Evie. "That's more than enough."

They took back their hands and beamed at each other. As long as the four of them were friends, anything was possible. The future was waiting.

"It was weird," said Mal. "There seemed to be something off about Celia."

"What?" asked Evie.

"Didn't you notice?" said Mal thoughtfully. "For a minute, it almost looked like she had no shadow."

Some
Time
Ago . . .

Lord of the Underworld

Okay, so maybe life on the Isle of the Lost wasn't too bad. There were still demons to do his bidding—fetch his coffee, run his errands, pick up his dry-cleaning. Sure, there wasn't any magic on the island, but henchmen abounded. Even Pain and Panic were there! And there was still food—spoiled and stale, of course, but edible. Oh, dear Athena, what was he saying? This place was a dump! A total nightmare! A low-rent establishment where even centaurs wouldn't stay! And they lived in *stables*!

He should be on Olympus, feasting on grapes, with nymphs hanging on his every word and laughing at all his jokes! Not scrounging for scraps in the back of an alley, just to have some uppity wicked fairy who thought she ran the place chastise him for being in her way.

Hades fumed until his face was red. His hair no longer burst into flame, which was probably a good thing, because nothing on the Isle was fire-retardant. He *had* to get out of here! He just had to find a way.

If he couldn't burst through the invisible barrier that surrounded the Isle of the Lost, or climb over it, there was only one way left: dig underneath it. After he'd fallen off the pirate-mast ladder, he had set his crew of demons, goblins, and pirates to digging as deep as they could, creating a maze of tunnels underneath the Isle of the Lost. Hades went down to see how the work was going.

"Any luck?" he asked. "Have we hit Auradon yet?"

"No," said a sweaty pirate, wiping his forehead with his bandanna and resting on his shovel. "Nothing."

"Maybe this way?" said Hades, gesturing over to the other direction.

"No, I think I hear water trickling from this way," argued the pirate.

"Hmmm. Okay," said Hades. (In fact, he had just missed the fork that led into the Endless Catacombs of Doom, which would be discovered and explored by a crew of young villains one day. But that's another story.)

Instead, they kept digging until they dug around in a complete circle. It was officially official: There was no way out of the Isle of the Lost.

Hades raged. He kicked the cave walls. He took his ember and began banging it on the walls of the tunnel, creating a single tiny crack. For a moment, a minuscule blue spark glared weakly from deep within the crack, but it died out before Hades even noticed.

"BY ZEUS, THIS IS IMPOSSIBLE!" he screamed.

Then he called the biggest and strongest demons back and made them clean up the largest part of the tunnel that he would take as his cave. If he was going to be stuck here, he might as well be comfortable. Every good villain needed a lair.

Caps & Gowns

"My heart is
telling me that
we are not
our parents."
—Mal,
Descendants

chapter
37

Auradon or Auradon't

On Monday morning, the students of Dragon Hall gathered for their regular assembly in the crumbling auditorium before classes began. Except there was nothing regular about this morning's assembly at all. In fact, it was completely *irregular*, because no one had ever actually adhered to the morning schedule, instead just showing up late or causing trouble in the hallways. So when an announcement boomed in the overhead speakers that attendance was mandatory, the students knew something was up.

Dizzy and Celia found seats in the front and waited to hear the news with the rest of the school. Dr. Facilier slunk into the room, and a hush fell over the crowd. Some of the younger first-years began to shake and tremble. The witch doctor headmaster was downright frightening sometimes, with his eyes that seemed to see through your soul. Celia should know—it was the look he gave her when she used up the last bit of expired milk in the morning and then put the jug back in the fridge.

"Good morning, villains," Dr. Facilier greeted them when he stepped up to the microphone, a sneering Professor Tremaine and a clueless Coach Gaston behind him. "I have some special news."

He surveyed the crowd. "Transfer applications to Auradon Prep will be available today. These students will be able to leave the Isle of the Lost this summer and continue their studies in Auradon."

Auradon!

Wasn't this what Mal was saying the other day? From the balcony? That was real? It wasn't a trap after all? And that roundtable discussion they had invited everyone to (except almost no one went) . . . that was also legit?

"The students who are chosen will be celebrated throughout the land and enjoy a spectacular welcome feast at the school, complete with a parade. Your names will be immortal, and you will be known throughout the kingdom as the Isle's finest villains," said Dr. Facilier, playing directly to the crowd.

"Remember, only the wickedest of you will be chosen,"

he added with a laugh. "Auradon representatives will be back in a few weeks to announce their selections for the VK program. Now go forth and do your evil deeds."

Celia and Dizzy turned to each other, almost unable to contain their excitement. They were really taking applications! They could really go to Auradon Prep! They clasped hands and headed to the front, where the application forms were stacked.

"My dad said they're going to take four kids," said Celia.

"Only four?" asked Dizzy. "That's not that many."

"There are only two of us!" said Celia. "We'll make it."

"Evie said they're going to come back to the Isle again in a few weeks," said Dizzy. "That must have been what your dad meant when he mentioned the Auradon representatives. Maybe they'll bring us back then!"

"Maybe."

"And the celebration sounds amazing," said Dizzy. "A welcome feast!"

"I hope it's a warm welcome," Celia said with a snicker.

There was a bevy of students fighting over the applications.

"You're applying?" Dizzy asked, as she saw her cousin Anthony Tremaine take a form.

"Why not?" said Anthony, raising an eyebrow. "At least in Auradon there's better hair gel."

Ginny Gothel walked up with her friend Harriet Hook.

"I'll take one," said Ginny, her curly black hair flowing down her back. "There's magic in Auradon. Even if it's regulated, I want to see what I can do there. What about you, Harriet?"

"My sister CJ likes it there, so I'm a little curious," said Harriet. "But Harry would never move to Auradon, not without his pirates."

Ginny nodded. She couldn't imagine Harry without his crew. He was practically miserable without his captain, Uma. "So are you going to apply or not?"

"I'm not sure," said Harriet. "Maybe. Fine, I'll take one. Actually, give me three, I'm babysitting for the Smees tonight. Maybe their kids want to apply."

By the time the bell rang for the first class, almost all the applications had been taken.

chapter

38

Building a Brand

It was a few weeks after their return from the Isle of the Lost, and things were starting to gear up for graduation, which was coming faster than Cinderella's carriage trying to get home before midnight. During the debriefing, Ben asked the four of them if they thought the visit was a success, and they had unanimously agreed that they had done their best. Ben had assured them that was all he had hoped for, and Mal, Evie, Carlos, and Jay went back to focusing on enjoying the last days of the school year.

Just as Doug had predicted, almost all the graduating seniors of Auradon Prep wanted an Evie's 4 Hearts original cap and gown for the ceremony. Between finals and trying to get all the gowns ready, Evie was so busy that Doug had to step in and help as business manager.

A line of girls stood in the hallway leading to Evie and Mal's room, waiting for their appointments. Doug walked out with a clipboard. "Okay, who's next? Oh, Ally, come on up."

Ally of Wonderland ran over. "Is it ready?" she asked upon entering the room, which resembled a high-end boutique.

"Almost," said Evie with a smile as she brought out Ally's blue-and-white gown. "Let's see it on you."

Ally popped into the changing room and walked out, radiant. "I love it!" she said, looking in the mirror. The gown's colors complemented her bright blue eyes and fair hair. "It's even perfect for a tea party!" she said, clapping her hands.

Jordan was next, and she approved her flowing, midriff-baring graduation gown with its matching silk cap. She modeled it for Evie and did a little dance. "It's gorgeous," Genie's daughter said. "Thanks, Evie."

"*You're* gorgeous," said Evie. "It's the girl, not the gown!"

"I can't believe we're finally graduating," said Jordan sadly. "I'll miss this place."

"Me too," said Evie. "It's not just a school—it's a home."

"What are your plans for after?" asked Jordan.

"More of this, I think," said Evie. "Designing. Maybe

doing a fashion show or two. There's so much to think about. What about you?"

Jordan shrugged. "I'm not sure yet. I'll probably travel the world with my dad for a while. Maybe leave my lamp somewhere and see if I feel like granting wishes."

"Good luck," said Evie, hugging her close.

"You too," said Jordan.

Ariana Rose, Audrey's snooty cousin, swanned in, casting a skeptical eye at Evie's establishment. "The three good fairies were supposed to make my graduation gown, but of course they're too busy with Audrey's," she said. "Audrey, Audrey, Audrey." She rolled her eyes in annoyance. "I mean, who cares about Audrey? She's not even dating Ben anymore. Or Chad."

"Did you want the blue or the pink?" Evie asked, holding up two gowns.

Ariana put her hands on her hips and almost stomped her feet. "Both, remember?"

Evie forced a smile. "Audrey doesn't have to date a prince to be happy."

"Wow, you're naïve," said Ariana. "Only a prince would make me happy!"

Evie wrapped up her gowns. "I used to think that too," she said.

"And now?"

Evie pressed the brown paper package holding the blue and pink gowns into Ariana's hands. "I'm just happy to have someone who cares about me."

Ariana sniffed. "Hmmpf."

Mal entered the room just as Ariana was leaving. "Oh, hey," said Mal. She wasn't a very popular person with Ariana's family.

Ariana merely brushed by Mal as if she didn't exist.

"You know how your mom cursed someone to sleep for a thousand years?" asked Evie.

Mal nodded.

"I totally get it now." Evie laughed.

Mal laughed with her, and for a moment, it felt fun to be just a little wicked.

Freddie was by far Evie's favorite client. Her graduation gown was red with black stripes. She adored the little top-hat cap that Evie had made her, complete with bone necklace. "This is bomb," said Freddie, looking at herself in the mirror. "You are a real magician, Evie."

"Thanks," said Evie modestly.

"Heard you guys saw my little sister Celia when you guys were back on the Isle," said Freddie. "How is she?"

"Good," said Evie. "She tried to read my fortune."

"Ha! Did you let her?" asked Freddie. "I hope not!"

• • •

Even Lonnie stopped by. Evie explained that her gown had pockets for her swords and a sheath for her bow and arrow too. "I wanted the gowns to be both fashionable *and* functional," said Evie.

"Extraordinary," said Lonnie. "I'll show my mom. Maybe she'll put in an order for the rest of the army." She drew Evie in for a hug. "I'm going to miss you," said Lonnie. "I can't believe we're all going to be separated so soon."

"I know, I'll miss you too," said Evie. "We won't be too far away, right? You'll come visit?"

"It's about a four-day carriage ride from the Imperial Palace to Auradon City," said Lonnie. "So we can't just pop in. But yes, I'll definitely come visit."

Evie promised she would too. Still, she knew that Lonnie was right—their visits would be few and far between. As much as she hated to admit it, this phase of their life was coming to a close. It was time to forge their own paths now.

Once more, Evie felt a rush of gratitude that she had been able to leave the Isle of the Lost and come to Auradon. Evie hoped that one day every little kid who grew up on that island would have the same opportunity.

Lonnie left and Jane knocked on the door. She was holding her trusty clipboard.

"Hey," said Evie. "I have your dress ready."

Jane didn't need a graduation gown, but Evie had made her a new dress for the occasion anyway. She brought it out—a silvery-blue cocktail dress with a pretty lace collar. "Evie, it's beautiful," said Jane in an awed voice. "It's the most beautiful dress I've ever seen."

Evie blinked back tears. "I'm so glad you love it."

"We'll miss you guys so much," Jane said, enveloping Evie in a deep hug.

"We'll be back tons," said Evie. "You'll be sick of us."

"Really, really sick, okay?" cried Jane. "So sick we have the flu."

"Promise," said Evie.

At the end of the week, Doug showed Evie his spreadsheet. "Look how much you earned! You are a queen!"

"Oh my fairest!" said Evie. "I can finally afford what I've wanted all this time!"

chapter

39

The Future's So Bright . . .

wo weeks before the very last day of school was the annual Senior Dinner, hosted by the royal family in honor of the graduating class. Ben came to knock on Mal's door to escort her to the event. He looked particularly dashing in a new blue-and-gold tuxedo that matched his crown. "Are you ready?" he asked.

Mal tucked her hair behind her ears and took one last look in the mirror. She was wearing a new purple dress trimmed with black lace that Evie had made her and had combed her hair just the way Dizzy had taught her. She hoped she had gotten it right. Doug and Evie had already left for the event just a few minutes earlier. When she turned to Ben, his smile widened.

"You look beautiful," he said.

"You don't look too bad yourself," she teased.

She took his arm and they made their way out of the dorms toward the main lawn, which had been set up with a majestic white tent for the night. Their fellow seniors milled around in their finest formal wear. Lonnie and Jay were standing by the buffet table, sampling the canapés. Jay was wearing his rust-colored Agrabah-style leather jacket with the epaulets. Carlos and Jane were talking to Fairy Godmother. Doug and Evie were once again saying hi to Doug's many cousins. (His dad did have six brothers.)

"Did I ever tell you how glad I am that nothing bad happened on the Isle this time?" said Ben, as he walked her to their table.

"About that," said Mal.

"Something bad happened?"

"Yes," she said. "Except I don't remember exactly what it was. We did get away. But we need to be vigilant. Something wicked this way comes. . . ."

Ben raised his eyebrows. "I'll double security right now."

"And we really did our best to try to convince kids to apply here," said Mal.

"I know you did."

"I just hope it was enough."

"What's the event you're planning with Evie? VK Day? That sounds pretty cool," said Ben.

"I hope it works," said Mal.

"We'll be inundated with applications. You'll see," said Ben.

King Beast and Queen Belle arrived, and everyone took their seats. Mrs. Potts had outdone herself: there was hearty beef ragout, a bubbling and airy cheese soufflé, luscious and crispy roast chickens, mashed potatoes that had little pools of melted butter. It was the most decadent and delicious meal they ever had.

She was glad that Carlos and Jane had joined them, even though, technically, they were juniors. But as Carlos said, *technically*, Jane had planned the entire thing, down to the six-course dessert menu, so it was only fair that they got to attend.

Ben—who, in addition to being Auradon's king, was also the Class King—stood up to make a toast. "To the best Auradon Prep class ever!" he said. "My family wishes you all a wonderful future."

"To the future!" said Jay, smiling at Lonnie.

"The future!" said Evie, clinking glasses with Doug.

"The future!" said Mal, who feverishly hoped it brought only peace and no threats from her homeland.

"To your future!" said Carlos, nudging Jay while he took a big sip from his glass.

"My future indeed!" said Jay. "I'm going to check out Sherwood Forest University this weekend for visiting day."

"You've decided?" asked Lonnie.

"Not yet. I want to check it out, but I'm excited to see what it's all about."

"Take care," said Ben. "They get pretty merry over there. But I'm sure you can handle it."

Over dessert, Evie told them her good news. "So, you know how I've been making caps and gowns for everyone? I earned enough money to buy a place of my own. A home in Auradon," she said.

"Oh, Evie!" said Mal, reaching across the table to give her friend a hug. "That's amazing!"

"Wow, your own pad, huh? Sweet," said Jay, looking a bit jealous.

"It's perfect! We found this tiny little adorable cottage in the woods," said Evie.

"We?" said Mal with a raised eyebrow. She elbowed Ben, who covered a smile with his goblet.

"Doug helped me find it! His uncle was the listing agent," said Evie quickly. "Who knew Doc wasn't a doctor? He's in real estate."

"Is he, now?" asked Jay, who raised his glass in Doug's direction while Doug blushed and coughed.

"What?" Evie asked with wide eyes.

"Mmm-hmm," said Mal with a smirk.

Evie ignored her friends' teasing, and Doug tried to look somewhere else, even as his ears turned crimson.

"Evie, ignore them," said Carlos, reaching to hold Jane's hand.

Evie nodded. She was all business. "Anyway, as I was saying, this solves our problem! The four new villain kids can stay with me over the summer. There's a ton of space."

Carlos stole a bite of Jane's cake. Then he turned to Ben. "Hey, I just realized—Jane and I will still be here at school next year. So we can mentor the new villain kids!"

"Can we?" said Jane.

"It'll be like having a bunch of little brothers and sisters!" said Carlos.

"Okay." Jane laughed. "Whatever you want."

"It's all settled, then," said Mal. "They'll stay with Evie this summer, and Jane and Carlos will help them out."

"Perfect," said Evie, looking very pleased.

"Now we just need four kids to apply," Jay reminded them.

Ben pushed his slice of cake over to Carlos so he would stop eating Jane's. "Don't worry, they will."

chapter
40

Decisions, Decisions

When Jay arrived at Sherwood Forest University, he was greeted by a friendly student dressed in the green livery of the school. "Hey, man, I'm Bobby Hood," he said. "Welcome to Sherwood."

"Your dad is a legend," said Jay, bumping his fist. "You're a student here?"

"My first year," said Bobby with a grin. "Come on, let me show you around."

Bobby gave Jay the campus tour—taking him to the archery fields, the student center, and the academic buildings. "And here's the R.O.A.R. gym," he said. "It's where you'll be playing."

It was a gleaming indoor gymnasium, filled with R.O.A.R. athletes in green uniforms, leaping off the walls and practicing with their swords and shields. Jay grinned. "Excellent."

Next, Jay sat in on a few lectures. The history classes were mostly concerned with the medieval and Renaissance periods, and an economics class showed how taking money from the wealthy aided the less fortunate.

"But of course, the best thing here is the merrymaking," said Bobby. "Come on."

He led Jay to the middle of the forest, where a few students were strumming guitars, playing games, and generally goofing off. There was a group of merry men who looked like a cheeky, irreverent bunch. And they definitely seemed like they were good with their bows and arrows.

"So, what do you think?" said Bobby.

"It's awesome," said Jay. If he chose to enroll at Agrabah State University, he would be burdened by his father's legacy. Magical Institute Training was prestigious, but sounded way too academic and, well, magical for him—and he wasn't very good at magic. Sherwood Forest U seemed like the perfect fit.

"Good luck," said Bobby, shaking his hand. "Hope to see you here next year!"

Jay realized with a start that he still had to get in. Even though he was recruited and invited, nothing was set in stone until he received his admission scroll. Suddenly, he knew exactly how Dizzy felt about her Auradon application.

• • •

At last, it was the very end of school. Final grades had been posted, and graduation was only a few days away. It was also the week in which college decisions would go out to those who had applied. Some people had applied early and already knew where they were headed. Lonnie was going pro, joining her brother on the Great Wall team. Evie was expanding her fashion line. Mal was going to help Ben with his royal duties and learn the ropes of palace life.

But Jay still hadn't heard back from all of his schools.

Early digital acceptances, as well as fat envelopes from both MIT and ASU, had arrived. Jay had his heart set on Sherwood Forest University, though. Yet ever since he'd returned from visiting day the other week, there had been no word from the school or the coach.

Now he had to wait with everyone else in the library, staring at a computer, refreshing his screen to see if he had been accepted to the school of his choice.

Jay drummed his fingers on the desk nervously. He never thought he'd ever graduate from high school, let alone go to college. Growing up on the Isle of the Lost, he didn't think he had much of a future. But all that had changed when he came to Auradon. His whole life was ahead of him now. In the end, he told himself, it would be okay if he didn't get into Sherwood. There were other schools. What was important was that he was going to get to do something that he loved, no matter where he ended up.

He refreshed the screen.

There it was. There was a message!

CLICK HERE FOR APPLICATION DECISION

Jay hit the button and bit his thumb. He never had to wait for anything in his life. For so many years, if he wanted something, he just took it, or stole it, or talked his way into it. If he got in, this would be one of the first times he had actually earned something.

JAY OF AGRABAH, CONGRATULATIONS!
YOU HAVE BEEN ACCEPTED INTO SHERWOOD FOREST
UNIVERSITY'S MERRY BAND OF STUDENTS. . . .

It was even signed by Robin Hood himself.

He leaped to his feet and yelled, "I'm going to college!"

Carlos came over and slapped him on the back. "Congratulations, man! Dude and I are so happy for you!"

"Go, Jay!" said Evie, who had been sitting with Doug. Doug was still waiting to hear whether he had gotten into one of the top seven schools in the kingdom. They both stood up and hugged Jay.

"You did it!" said Mal, jumping up and down with Ben, as other kids began to scream out their acceptances.

It was a frenzy of excitement and relief. Students tossed their books and notebooks around and danced on the tables.

"I'm sad you're not going pro with me," said Lonnie. "But I'll come visit you."

"Thanks. And I'll come see you when you guys play at Sherwood Arena," said Jay.

"Perfect," said Lonnie.

Jay grinned. His future gleamed brighter than all the gold in the world.

chapter

41

Ways to Be Wicked

*E*ven at Auradon Prep, senior year meant a certain loosening of the rules. Fairy Godmother didn't look askance at seniors slouching in late to classes, or leaving their spells unchecked. Earlier in the year, when Mal heard of another secret tradition, the Senior Prank, she decided that the four former villains had to mastermind this operation.

"It's the Senior Prank, and we're from the Isle of the Lost!" she told Evie, Jay, Ben, and Carlos, who was helping too.

"Oh, we've got this," said Jay, punching a fist into his palm in excitement.

"We'll make sure they'll never forget us!" said Evie.

"After we pull this off, they might want to," said Carlos.

"What exactly do you have in mind?" asked Ben, who couldn't help but look a little worried.

So on the very last day of school, when Auradon students left the dorms for the academic buildings, they found a carriage crashed into the front of the school entrance. The carriage was half in and half out of the wall, and part of it was made of pumpkin. It looked like something terrible had happened.

People gasped until they read what was written on the back of the carriage window, where Mal had scrawled SENIORS RULE!

But there was more. All the vending machines were stocked with water bottles that just happened to have goldfish inside of them. The hallways were either filled with balloons or covered in plastic wrap. Every chair in the cafeteria had been switched out for a throne and turned upside down. A New Orleans jazz band followed Fairy Godmother around all day.

"Senior Prank," the professors said with a sigh.

The seniors laughed.

Jay and Carlos hoisted up a large FOR SALE sign on top of the school's roof, while Evie and Mal drew a colorful chalk mural depicting all the seniors on the front concrete steps.

Mal put the finishing touches on Ben's crown and looked at Evie. "I can't believe it's over."

"Me neither," said Evie. "We had so much fun."

"Remember when we first got here? How nervous we were?" said Mal.

"Audrey was so mean to you!" said Evie, shaking her head.

"All we wanted to do was wreck the place," said Mal.

"I'm so glad we didn't," said Evie.

"Yeah, me too," said Mal.

The boys slid down from the roof and admired the mural. "Nice picture of Dude," said Carlos happily.

"Dude is definitely a senior," said Mal.

"Yeah, he's graduating with us," said Evie. "Even if you're staying."

"You guys, it's over," said Carlos, his voice hoarse. "You're leaving Auradon Prep. What are we going to do without you?"

Mal felt tears come to her eyes. "We'll always be friends," she said, slinging an arm around Evie.

"Always," said Evie, embracing her back.

"Always," said Jay, putting an arm around both of them.

"I'm not going anywhere," said Carlos. "I have one more year!" Then he laughed and joined the group hug. "Always."

chapter

42

Pomp and Circumstance

$\mathcal{M}$al couldn't believe it was finally here: Graduation Day! The tents had been set up, and the parents and grandparents and friends and sidekicks had arrived. So many carriages had rolled up to Auradon Prep that morning, it had caused a bit of a traffic jam. Aladdin and Jasmine were there, looking proud of Aziz. Cinderella and Prince Charming were taking many pictures of Chad, who kept blinking in every photo. The whole Rose family came too: Queen Leah, Princess Aurora, Prince Philip, all fussing around Audrey, who looked radiant, while her cousin Ariana pouted next to her.

Carlos stood at the entrance, looking handsome in

his black-and-white morning suit, handing out programs. "Welcome to Auradon Prep."

The first strains of the baccalaureate song played: *Auradon, fair and true . . . Auradon, gold and blue . . . Auradon, for me and you . . .*

The seniors walked in, led by Ben in his cap and gown, holding Mal's hand. Evie was next, with Doug and Jay falling in step behind her.

Carlos held up his camera. "Say hi to the Isle!"

"The Isle?" asked Mal.

"Yes! Surprise!" said Jane, holding up a microphone. "This is the surprise we were working on! Everyone on the Isle can watch you guys graduate!"

"To inspire every little villain kid! We wanted them to be able to see that they can grow up to do amazing things one day, just like all of you have," said Carlos.

"That's awesome!" said Mal. She turned to Ben. "Did you know about this?"

He grinned. "I helped set up the streaming signal."

Mal waved to the camera. "Hi, everyone! Apply to Auradon Prep! We'd love to have you!"

The graduating seniors took their seats, and Fairy Godmother welcomed everyone. "Students, parents, princes and princesses, fairies and sultans, kings and queens. We are so proud of this class!" she said. "We have been through a lot together, and now we celebrate your accomplishments! This is a momentous day for you all. Now I'd like to introduce someone who makes us all proud to live in Auradon— King Ben!"

A huge storm of applause rained down from the crowd as Ben came up to the podium. He smiled at his subjects. "Thank you, Fairy Godmother! I'm so proud to welcome you all here today, to our graduation. I'm not just your king—I'm also a new graduate. I'm proud to call you all my friends, and I'm even prouder to introduce the person who was voted this year's class speaker. Mal, of the Isle of the Lost!"

There was another roar of applause. Evie, Jay, Carlos, and Doug jumped to their feet and gave Mal a standing ovation as she walked to the stage.

Mal stepped up to the microphone. "When I first arrived at Auradon Prep, I was definitely its worst student. I used my magic for selfish reasons. I even cast a spell on Ben because I wasn't sure if he liked me."

Ben leaned over and whispered, "I always liked you."

Mal smiled. "That wasn't all. My friends and I even tried to steal Fairy Godmother's wand, so that we could free everyone on the Isle of the Lost, including our parents."

There was a slight titter from the crowd. Fairy Godmother shifted in her seat, but gave Mal an encouraging smile.

Mal continued. "But being a student here at Auradon Prep, I learned that good is better than evil. I learned to make friends. I learned to love. I learned I don't have to be a certain kind of person because I was born in a certain part of the world. I can be anyone I want to be. I can be strong, and I can be weird, and I can be myself. That's what I learned in Auradon—that I can change for the better. We all can. Change is good. Because we are all in it together, and only together can we change the world and make it a better place. We are now alumni of Auradon Prep. Let's go out there and make some magic!"

This time, the entire audience gave Mal a standing ovation.

"I'm so proud of Mal," said Jane, wiping away tears. "I'm so proud of all of them!"

"You did an amazing job planning the entire thing," said Carlos. "Your birthday's coming up, right?"

"It was yesterday," said Jane.

Carlos paled. "It was?!"

Jane laughed and gave him a hug. "I'm only kidding. Yes, it's coming up soon."

Carlos sighed in relief. He had some planning of his own to do.

chapter

43

Auradon Alums

At last, it was time for the main event. Fairy Godmother called up each student one by one to hand them their diploma. King Beast shook each graduate's hand, and Queen Belle handed them a gold-embossed Auradon Prep pin in the shape of a book. Ally of Wonderland was first, then Arabella, King Triton's grand-daughter. The Rose girls were next: Ariana and Audrey, who wore matching pouts, followed by a cocky Aziz.

"King Ben," called Fairy Godmother with a proud smile.

"Congratulations, son," said his father, with a firm handshake.

"We're so thrilled," whispered his mother, giving him a kiss on the cheek.

Ben grinned and walked off the stage, showing his pin to Mal, who helped fasten it to his lapel.

Doug was next. He waved his diploma up in the air and whistled as he walked back to his seat.

"Evie," called Fairy Godmother.

Evie curtsied to the dignitaries before joining her friends back in the audience.

Jay was next, and he raised his fist in victory upon receiving his diploma, and ran up the walls before jogging off the stage.

"And now we present the commencement awards," said Fairy Godmother. "For most improved student: Mal."

Mal blushed as she received her award. "Me?"

"Who else?" said Fairy Godmother with a wink. The next award was for best athlete, which went to Jay, who did a backflip upon receiving it.

"The award for diligence goes to none other than Evie," said Fairy Godmother. Doug cheered the loudest when Evie walked up to receive it.

The ceremony concluded, and the seniors filed out of the auditorium to a fireworks show.

"What's next?" wondered Jay, as they stopped to admire the fiery display that lit up the sky over Castle Beast.

"Everything," said Ben, with his arm slung around Mal. "Anything."

"Maybe we could travel Auradon together," said Mal.

"That could be arranged, my lady," said Ben.

"We still need to keep an eye out for Uma," said Mal.

"We will," promised Ben. "We'll keep Auradon safe, together."

Carlos and Jane walked up to join them. "What a big day!" he said.

Evie sighed happily, hand in hand with Doug, but at Carlos's words she straightened. "No! The big day is coming up soon!" said Evie.

"What's bigger than graduation?" asked Jay.

"VK Day!" said Evie. "It's going to be huge!"

"That's right," said Ben. "Fairy Godmother said they're inundated with applications from the Isle of the Lost."

Mal, Evie, Jay, and Carlos turned to each other with gleeful smiles.

"More villains, huh?" said Mal. "Are you sure Auradon can handle them?"

"More than sure," said Ben. "We've got you guys to show them the ropes!"

"We've got to get ready to welcome them!" said Evie.

"Don't worry. We'll make sure to roll out the purple carpet," said Mal.

Then together, they made their way to the graduation reception to celebrate their hard-earned accomplishments.

Once upon a time, four villain kids from the Isle of the Lost came to Auradon with wicked intentions, but today, they were graduating as some of the kingdom's bravest and best subjects.

Mal squeezed Ben's hand, thinking she was the luckiest girl in the world, especially when she looked over at her friends—sweet Evie, strong Jay, smart Carlos. She wouldn't be where she was without them. They were all in this together. They had all grown up so much, and now they were ready for whatever else was in store.

Rotten to the core? Maybe not so rotten anymore!

epilogue

Ocean Pollution

The force that propelled Mal up and out of the waves had also pushed Uma away from the pirate ship, sending her crashing against the rocks. She couldn't remember what had happened next, only that she had been rescued by her mother's loyal pets, Flotsam and Jetsam, who nudged her awake.

They swam away once they saw her eyes flutter open.

But Uma was confused. Where was she? What was she doing?

What just happened?

She had come so close to winning something, but what? Why couldn't she remember? Her head was throbbing.

Then she heard it: loud, blaring rock music.

Hades!

Now she remembered: She and Hades had a deal. They were going to go after Mal. Bring her down, bring the barrier down, win their freedom, and escape from the Isle of the Lost once and for all!

Uma swam up to the cave, looking for the fissures in the stone where she had slipped inside the tunnel. But everything was plugged up with a dense, solid material, dark and shining. It repelled her touch, sending her back into the water.

"Hades!" Uma screamed. *"Hades!* Let me in!"

But there was no answer.

There was no way for Uma to shape-shift into a form that would allow her to slip through the cracks, because there were no cracks anymore.

That washed-up rock god had double-crossed her! But why? Was he on Mal's side now? What was that all about?

"Hades!" Uma raged. "You'll pay for this!"

This was all Mal's doing! She had won again. But one day, Uma vowed, she would have her revenge. She would show that purple-haired punk once and for all. Mal would never forget the name of the person who ruled the Isle of the Lost. The one who would bring Auradon to its knees.

Uma!

TO FIND OUT WHAT HAPPENS NEXT . . .

premieres Summer 2019

acknowledgments

A huge Auradon-style thank-you to my amazing editors, Hannah Allaman and Emily Meehan, for their faith and patience. Thank you to my family at Disney Publishing Worldwide, especially Guy Cunningham, Meredith Jones, Dan Kaufman, Seale "Eddy" Ballenger, Dina Sherman, MAZ!, Elena Blanco, Kim Knueppel, Elke Villa, Holly Nagel, and Andrew Sansone. Thank you to our Disney queen, Tonya Agurto.

Thank you to our partners at Disney Channel, especially Gary Marsh, Jennifer Rogers-Doyle, and Miriam Ogawa. Thank you to the director and stars of *Descendants 3*: Kenny Ortega, Dove Cameron, Mitchell Hope, Sofia Carson,

Cameron Boyce, Booboo Stewart, Brenna D'Amico, Zachary Gibson, Sarah Jeffery, and Jedidiah Goodacre.

Thank you to my 3Arts family, Richard Abate and Rachel Kim.

It's been such a fun ride. Thank you to my two favorite people on the planet: my husband, Mike, and our daughter, Mattie, for putting up with the late nights and grumpy days. Thank you to my DLC family, especially my nephews Nicholas, Josey, and Seba, and my niece Marie. Thank you to all my dear friends, especially those who were so nice every time I had to cancel plans because I was on deadline.

Thank you to all the amazing Descenders and the people who maintain the Descendants Isle of the Lost books Wiki. WOW! You guys were an amazing help every time I had to look up something in the earlier books!

So much love, your loyal scribe,

Melissa (Mel) de la Cruz • February 2019

Los Angeles, CA

Sometimes being good ISN'T SO BAD

BOOK ONE

BOOK TWO

BOOK THREE

BOOK FOUR